Queens
PARK

Queen's
PARK
A Detective Lane Mystery

GARRY RYAN

Gary and Marilyn

Hope you,
enjoy!

Garry
Ryan

NEWEST
PRESS

Library and Archives Canada Cataloguing in Publication
Ryan, Garry, 1953-
Queen's Park : a Detective Lane mystery / Garry Ryan.

ISBN 1-896300-84-7

I. Title. PS8635.Y35Q84 2004   C813'.6   C2004-903618-1

Board editor: Douglas Barbour
Author photograph: Karma Ryan
Cover photograph: Garry Ryan
Cover design: Ruth Linka
Interior design: Marijke Friesen

 Canada Council   Conseil des Arts   Canadian   Patrimoine   edmonton
for the Arts   du Canada   Heritage   canadien   arts
                                                                                      council

NeWest Press acknowledges the support of the Canada Council for the
Arts and the Alberta Foundation for the Arts, and the Edmonton Arts
Council for our publishing program. We also acknowledge the financial
support of the Government of Canada through the Book Publishing
Industry Development Program (BPIDP) for our publishing activities.

NeWest Press
201–8540–109 Street
Edmonton, Alberta T6G 1E6
(780) 432-9427
www.newestpress.com

1 2 3   4 5 07 06 05 04

PRINTED AND BOUND IN CANADA

For
Sharon,
Karma,
and
Ben
with love
and
gratitude.

CHAPTER 1

"I'm uneasy when 140 kilos up and disappears," Lane said, glancing at the line in the downtown coffee shop. It stretched to the door. He took a grateful sip from his cappuccino.

Lisa said, "Just started digging on this one. Where are you, anyway?"

"Having a coffee." He knew she was sitting at her desk, her RCMP uniform ironed just right, every short blond hair in place as she sat at attention. Ever since he'd known Lisa, she'd carried herself like a soldier. "The Swatsky case makes me feel like we're always playing catch-up. Something could be happening right now. If we're lucky, we'll find out about it in a month."

"That's one reason why we keep in touch. Gives us a chance to catch up. What's your next step?" Lisa asked.

"Think I'll see the grandmother. She was in the house when it happened."

"What about the boy?"

"Hard to say. Only he knows how much he can remember. After what happened, the kid has to be in shock or denial."

"What's his name again?"

"Ernie," Detective Lane said.

"That's right. I'll keep you posted. We still on for Tuesday?"

"Yep. Loraine coming?"

"She wouldn't miss it. Loraine always likes an opportunity to analyze. She's says you're enigmatic."

"Arthur can help her with her analysis while you and I talk shop," Lane said.

"See you then," Lisa said and hung up.

❧

"Calgary, sixty-two kilometres," Marvin said.

"Oh shit, do you have to read every goddamned sign along the highway?" Lester said.

"How'd you get the gun?" Marvin asked while reaching down the front of his pants.

"Would you quit playin' with yourself?" Lester said.

"Gettin' hot in here." Marvin eased his balls up and away from thick thighs. "Ahh," Marvin pulled one hand out and aimed the vent between his legs. "How'd you get the gun?"

"Freddy." A semi passed them on the left. It pushed a wave of air into their lane. Lester gripped the wheel tighter.

"Freddy who?" Marvin said.

"Freddy whose wife left him. She wanted alimony. I took the rifle out one night. Put a bullet through her kitchen window. The old lady got the message. Saved Freddy some money and he brought a Smith and Wesson nine millimetre Sigma back from the States." He patted the holster under his left arm.

"Let me see," Marvin said.

"No way."

"How come?" Marvin lifted his knees and rested them against the dash.

"You're so stupid, you'll shoot a hole in something."

"Not stupid enough to trust Bob," Marvin said.

"I had to sign those papers!"

"For half, right?" Marvin said.

"That's right. Half a million."

"Your name's on all the documents. The newspapers say Bob stole over 3 million. Half of 3 million is not $500,000."

Lester lifted his sports jackets to reveal the butt of the pistol. "Mr. Smith and Mr. Wesson will help us find Bob."

"If the cops can't find him, what makes you think we can?"

"Think," Lester tapped his temple. "Mom always said you were a few bricks short of a load. The last place he was seen was the old lady's. Papers make it sound like Bob disappeared after screwin' golden boy."

"Golden boy?"

"The old lady's favourite grandchild. Judy was always pissed because golden boy got the best of everything," Lester said.

"So, what do we need the old lady for?"

"Think! Judy's gone. Bob's disappeared. The old lady's still there. We go talk to her and the kid. See what we can find out."

"She's not gonna talk to us," Marvin said.

"She won't have a choice when I shove a gun into golden boy's mouth!"

"What's his name?"

"Whose name, you stupid son of a bitch?"

"Golden boy's," Marvin said.

"Ernie."

CHAPTER 2

"He calls it his mate," fifteen-year-old Ernie dropped into the swivelling recliner facing the fireplace.

"I don't know how you can ride in the back seat with that doll in the front." Nanny took a quick gulp of oxygen. Her face was a geological map of a life in shades of cookie dough. She lifted the clear plastic oxygen tubing over silver hair and dropped it. The tube left grooves in the flesh on her face.

"Nanny . . ." Ernie said.

She reached for the pack of menthols. Curling her hand around the lighter, she flicked the wheel. With the cigarette between two hooked fingers, she lit and inhaled. Her eyes widened as the nicotine filled what remained of her lungs. "I think it's sick paying $6,000 for a doll." Her voice was a rasp on oak, tearing away at each word. "He's got better things to spend his money on."

Ernie rubbed his palms on denim. "Says she never talks back, never tells him how to drive, and doesn't say anything when he picks his nose."

"He should put some clothes on her if he's gonna take her wherever he goes." Nanny took a pull on the cigarette.

He picked a dog hair from his black T-shirt. "Says she understands his problems."

"Sick old bastard! Why do you have to tell me all of this?"

"Because you always ask." He leaned back in the chair and crossed his legs.

"Heard the news about your uncle?" She pronounced the "your" as if Bob Swatsky was Ernie's fault.

He rubbed the bruise on his left cheek and wondered how long it would take to fade.

"Police found your Uncle Bob's car and they're still looking for the money." Nanny nodded in the direction of the TV. "Mute" was written across the bottom of a man's belly, as he bit into a hot dog dripping ketchup, onions, and mustard. He smiled and chewed while gripping the bun with thick fingers.

⚬

Ernie's eyes slid out of focus as the flashback filled his mind. Uncle Bob's sausage fingers gripped Ernie high on the thigh. Then, fingers pulled at Ernie's belt. A knife blade ran across the bridge of Ernie's nose. The smell of onions on Bob's breath. Ernie focused on the open collar of his uncle's white shirt and the hollow at his throat. Ernie's free right hand automatically crossed forefinger over index; the way he'd been trained to do it in karate. He pulled his elbow back. A roll of flesh sagged beneath Bob's chin.

"On your knees," Bob said.

Ernie struck. Both fingertips disappeared into the flesh at the base of Bob's throat. Bob gurgled and dropped the knife, put his hands to his throat and fell forward. His suffocating weight fell on top of Ernie. Bob's chin struck the boy on the cheek. His head hit the oak floor.

⚬

Ernie heard Scout whimpering.

He looked to his right. The scratches on the glass sliding door were nearly a half a metre long. Behind them sat his dog with her rear legs to one side and front paws trembling to hold the pose. She whimpered some more. Second-hand smoke caught at the back of his throat.

"Aren't you going to let her in?" Nanny asked.

He stood. Grabbing the handle of the door, he looked down and saw the dog's tail sweeping the deck. He opened the glass. Scout jumped up. "Down!" he said. He pushed Scout back across the deck and sat in a white plastic chair. Scout sat next to him, lifting her chin so Ernie could scratch her throat. The dog's ears were miniature sails. They turned to catch the sound of the gate squeaking open. A growl grew in her throat. "Hey," Ernie stood up. The hair on the back of the dog's neck lifted. He caught the sound of heavy footsteps on the sidewalk. His heart pounded. He looked left, ready to escape into the house. He reached for the handle on the screen. His nostrils filled with the stench of fear, onions, and sweat.

"Hello there, Scout." The voice was friendly and commanding.

Scout backed up. A hand appeared, followed by the sleeve of a tweed sports jacket and the face of Detective Lane. His short hair was thinning on top. "Hi Ernie," he said. His knees crackled when he crouched to offer his open palm to the dog. She moved forward to sniff his clothing. He smiled at Ernie and said, "I guess she smells my dog."

Ernie reached for the sides of his chair, his legs like rubber.

"Sorry, I didn't mean to startle you."

Ernie wondered how the detective noticed how ruffled he was while looking at Scout.

The detective's eyes were dark brown. "Got some questions for your grandmother."

"Nanny, Detective Lane is here," Ernie said.

"What the hell does he want?"

Lane smiled broadly and walked towards the doorway. Another five centimetres in height and he would have to duck. Ernie spotted Lane's missing earlobe. "What happened?" He pointed a finger at the mangled ear.

Lane turned and lifted his left hand to the side of his head. "This? Domestic dispute." He pointed to the scratches on the glass door. "What happened here?"

"Scout . . ." Ernie said. The dog trotted over. "When Bob came after me, she tried to get in."

"YOU WANNA TALK OR NOT?" Nanny's voice was an engine without a muffler.

"Hello Leona," Lane said and slid open the screen door. Its wheels squealed as he closed it.

Scout dragged a paw across Ernie's knee. She rolled and he leaned to scratch the fur along her belly. "How come no one wants to ask me what happened?"

⚓

Inside, Lane sat down on the black slate ledge at the mouth of the fireplace. For a little over two seconds, his eyes took in a flat plastic container with a separate compartment for each day's medication. Kleenex, cigarettes, and lighters were scattered across the coffee table. He noted Leona seemed to be shrinking inside her blue jogging suit and wondered if she noticed how frantic Ernie was. The boy had a magazine cover Latino face. Ernie's beauty was a terrible gift, Lane decided.

Nanny blew smoke over the table top.

Lane studied the plastic tube at her feet. An oxygen machine hummed.

"Haven't blown up yet," Nanny wheezed.

"Can't imagine it would be a pleasant experience for Ernie."

"Leave him out of it." A clot of phlegm appeared on Leona's top lip and got caught in her mustache.

"I wasn't aware he was involved."

"He's done nothing."

"Didn't say he had."

Leona took a short sniff of oxygen, gathering herself, "Then, why are you here?"

"We can't find your son-in-law." Lane leaned forward now, putting his palms on the knees of his grey slacks.

"Bob'll turn up. Always does."

Lane considered the anger and regret woven into her reply. "Sounds like you wish he wouldn't."

"After what Bob's done to my family, why would I want him back?" The end of her cigarette glowed.

Lane leaned closer, "What did he do, exactly?"

Leona looked at him for a moment, considered the last quarter of the cigarette. She glanced over her shoulder, saw Ernie and began a personal litany of painful memories. "My daughter, Judy, was eighteen when she met Bob." She pointed an arthritic finger at Lane. Her voice rose in volume as emotion elbowed its way in between the words. She stabbed the filter tip into the ash tray. "We had our store then. Macleod's Hardware. It was our dream to own our own store. Saved for fifteen years. The dream lasted three." She leaned forward to put the oxygen tube back on. "Judy met Bob in grade twelve. Did you know she had a bad leg?"

"No."

"She did. God, that kid was always fighting. Her legs never seemed to work right and the kids used to pick on her somethin' terrible. Judy never had a boyfriend till Bob came along. I tried to tell her he was no good for her but . . . " She lifted her shoulders in a shrug, "Couldn't tell her a thing. She ran away three times. Bob would hang around the store with his big, tough friends, Lester and Marvin. They'd sit in the back of a pickup and just stare. We even had a break-in. Knew it was them but the RCMP couldn't prove a thing. Then the rumours started."

"Rumours?"

"Someone started the rumour we were cheating our customers and that's how come our daughter ran away. Business dropped off to nothin'. You ever lived in a small town?"

"No."

"We had to sell. Judy kept comin' back to the school to see Beth. She was only thirteen then. Kept it all to herself. Tore Beth up inside. She gained forty pounds in six months. All because of the upset. I was sick by that time. Ended up in the hospital and in bed for a month. Beth had to take care of me and do all the housework. The doctor told Beth if she ever ran away like Judy did, it'd kill me."

Chair legs scraped over wood. Lane glanced to his left. Ernie was standing.

"Don't know what I woulda done without her," Nanny said.

Lane watched as Ernie looked at his grandmother. The detective saw rage and wondered what was behind the boy's anger. Ernie jammed his feet into running shoes and grabbed the blue leash off the white table. Scout's tail wagged.

"Are you listenin'?" Leona said.

Lane nodded.

"What did I say, then?"

"You don't know what you would have done without Beth."

Leona's eyes held him for a minute—a silent challenge. "Didn't see my Judy for five years after that. Not until her baby was born. The visit lasted fifteen minutes before we started to fight. You know, if my brother was still alive he would have been able to help. Got killed in the war, though. Italy."

"I'm sorry," Lane said automatically and wondered where Ernie went when he was angry.

"After that, every time we got together with Judy I'd get in a fight with her or Bob would say somethin' to get me goin'."

"So, you wanted him dead?" He locked onto Leona's pupils, waiting for her reaction.

She stared back at him without blinking, took a gulp of air and wheezed, "You bet." She took another gulp of air, "Thought you said he disappeared."

"Do you know where Bob Swatsky is?"

"I'd bet he's crawled into a hole someplace." She reached for her cigarettes.

Lane noticed a slight dilation of the pupils but it wasn't enough to make him sure she was lying.

✻

"Doesn't she piss you off when she does that?" Ernie said to Scout.

She licked her lips and wagged her tail.

The leash bit into Ernie's hand, "Slow down!" He pulled and she faced him, tongue hanging. Her saliva evaporated when it hit the concrete. "Doesn't she piss you off?"

Scout sat, head tipped to one side, both front paws on the ground, one rear leg cocked under her rump, the other held out like an outrigger. Her tail swept the cement.

"I mean, Nanny tells the same story over and over. Makes me want to scream!"

Scout lifted her left paw.

Ernie reached down and took it in his hand. The calloused pads felt sandpaper cool against his palm. "She's always complaining about her asthma and emphysema, then she smokes."

Scout barked once.

"And she's always badmouthing Nonno."

The dog leaned into the leash.

Ernie dropped to one knee, stuffed a thumb into the back of one running shoe and pulled it over his heel. Switching feet, he repeated the procedure.

Scout pressed her nose against his.

Ernie stood and wiped the back of his hand across his face. The sun dragged its fingernails along his neck.

Walking side by side, they passed hedges, dodged sprinklers, and savoured the shade under trees.

Ernie glanced up the lawn to the brown screen door of a cream coloured bungalow. It was a glance as practised and automatic as putting one foot ahead of the other. He saw the picture window, then his eyes moved on to the two smaller bedroom windows. He tried to guess which one was Lesley's and hoped for a glimpse of her red hair. Lesley had grown up in that house. She had sat with Ernie in his grandfather's living room and watched television for two glorious hours.

Another flashback felt like a blow to Ernie's ribs. There was the knife blade at the bridge of his nose. Stainless steel was written on metal freshly licked by a whetstone. Uncle Bob Swatsky's thick fingers probed him. Then Ernie heard, "I'll cut your friggin' nose off if you don't ... " The whisper was as cold as the knife.

Is this what it'll be like from now on? Flashbacks of Bob crowding in on me? Ernie thought. Scout pulled him forward.

Up ahead, he spotted the Italian flag on the bumper of his grandfather's red Dodge van. Next to the flag was "I," a heart and "Italia." Inside the sidewalk, a two metre high hedge created a green wall around three sides of the front yard. Ernie followed Scout through a gap in the hedge. On the other side, two spruce trees stood fifteen metres high. Their branches touched. Scout turned left. Ernie reached over the white fence and opened the latch. Stepping down four stairs, he released the leash and lifted the branch of a raspberry bush. Thumb-sized berries hid there. Ernie closed his eyes and remembered the callouses of his father's hand, then his own thumb and forefinger picking the berries offered during long ago summers.

Deeper in the yard, next to the fence, a Cinzanno umbrella dropped a circle of shade over a table and three chairs. In one chair, with her back to him, wearing a pizza pan sized white straw hat and nothing else, sat the love doll. Her flesh was a healthy pink, her hair platinum blond, and all of her nails were painted red.

"Nonno?" Ernie said. He leaned forward, looked over the back step and around the corner of the house. His grandfather was on hands and knees, fingers guiding an orange marigold from its green plastic pot into a hollow dug in the loam at the edge of the garden. The back of Nonno's red and green T-shirt didn't quite meet up with his green cotton pants. A plumber's crack ran at right angles to his belt. Scout, trailing the snake of her leash, pranced up behind.

Ernie raised his right hand to signal the dog to stop. She paid no attention. Her nose had caught the scent of salt and sweat. Scout's tongue slipped out and travelled along the crack from belt buckle to shirt.

"Son a ma bitch!" Scout backed away with her tail tucked. The marigold was launched into the air. Nonno threw his arms out to catch it but it was too far away. He fell face first into nasturtiums, marigolds, and freshly turned earth.

Ernie felt something shift inside of him. A release of the tightness around his heart. For a moment he felt free of dread.

Nonno backed out of the garden. Keys and coins sang in the old man's pocket as he ran across the yard. "Ernie!"

The boy looked up to see his grandfather's nose blocking the sun. The old man's eyes were as brown as the soil on his hands.

"Ernie!" Nonno's fingers gripped the boy's shoulders.

Through the tears in Ernie's eyes, Nonno swam and laughter erupted in painful sobs. Ernie pointed helplessly at Nonno, "You . . . you."

"Son a ma bitch." The old man gripped the brim of his ball cap and slapped it against his thigh.

Ernie leaned back, laughing at the sky.

"You gotta watch that goddamn dog! Give me a friggin' heart attack!" Nonno jammed fists onto hips and cocked his head so the boy saw a thicket of hair inside each of his grandfather's nostrils.

Ernie wiped a sleeve across his eyes, "You looked so funny." He laughed some more.

"Good to hear you laughing."

The boy wiped a sleeve across his eyes.

"You want some wine?"

Ernie nodded.

Nonno turned.

A bee flew too close to Scout. She launched herself, hung in the air, curled back her lips, and bit down on the bug. It spun to the ground. The dog pounced.

"How come she does that?" Nonno said as he opened the screen door, stamped the earth from his shoes and stepped out of them.

"Maybe cause she never gets stung," Ernie said while pulling up a chair across from the doll. His eyes fell to the line of shadow running across the tops of her breasts where darker colours circled nipples. He crossed his legs, feeling the pressure of an erection.

"Say hello to your Nonna." Nonno stepped out the back door with index finger and thumb stuck into two glasses. The other hand held a wine bottle.

Shame and a strange kind of revulsion hit Ernie low in the belly. He looked at the old man and tilted his head to the left.

"Go on." Nonno set three glasses on the table. "Say hello to your Nonna, your grandmother."

"Hello, Nonna."

Nonno smiled and filled both glasses. Ernie caught the wine's rich scent and remembered the weekend they'd spent carrying, sorting, and pressing the grapes down in the basement where the air remained thick with fermentation. Grandfather held his glass up, allowing the sun to shine through the red. "Almost one year old." Nonno took a sip and smiled.

Ernie drank, catching the faint promise of the future at the tip of the tongue and the back of the throat.

"Good for the heart." The old man slapped a palm against his ribs then lifted his cap and wiped a sleeve across his forehead. "A hot one, today."

"The police are at Nanny's. What's going on?"

Nonno's eyes, deep set behind sagging skin, locked onto the boy. Then he looked at the doll. A breeze wiped blond hair across her face. Her blue eyes appeared to be focused on Scout. The dog was on her back attempting to catch her tail. Nonna's elbows rested on the arms of the chair, her hands open, thumbs angled away from fingers. "Your grandmother and I got it all figured out."

Ernie sipped at his wine and tried to avoid looking at her perfect breasts.

"Nonna tells me, 'The boy has his whole life ahead of him. Up to us to protect the boy.' That's what she says to me."

"But . . . " Ernie began.

The old man held up his hand to halt conversation. "Drink your wine." He pointed at the doll before pointing at himself, "Let us take care of the rest."

Ernie spotted the Swatsky's Ford logo. It was veiled by a layer of mustard-coloured dust collected at the rear of the grey Taurus. On the bumper, a blue sticker warned: This vehicle insured by Smith and Wesson.

Scout growled.

Ernie's mouth turned dry. He studied the men inside. They sat in the front seats. Their shoulders came within a finger's width of touching. The back of the driver's head was like wet, black plastic. Heat rose off the roof and made the air waver.

A cigarette arced out the nearest window and landed near Scout's nose. The butt rolled and caught in a crack in the cement.

The shock of Scout's lunge almost turned Ernie's elbow inside out. She hit the end of the leash. Bent at the waist, he stumbled behind her, struggling to rein her in. Scout rose up on her hind legs only centimetres from the open passenger window.

The tanned elbow of the man in the passenger's seat disappeared inside of the car. "What the hell?"

Ernie leaned back, reeled in the dog, and ended up sitting on the grass looking through the window at the passenger and driver. He grabbed Scout's collar with his right hand. The dog's rage telegraphed its way to Ernie's fingers. He stood up, then his mouth fell open when he saw the driver leaning forward. A gun flopped forward against the satin lining of his grey sports coat. "What's your problem, kid?" His face was round as a pizza. Ernie counted four chins. The guy in the passenger seat was bald.

"Nothin'," Ernie said. He pulled Scout away from the car. Sweat rolled down his ribs. He looked at the men through the windshield and studied the passenger whose eyebrows seemed to form one line.

"What you lookin' at?" The man leaned his head out the passenger window. Scout snarled.

Ernie smelled a mixture of sweat and garlic seeping out from inside the car. "Come on." He dragged Scout across the street. Her nails clawed the pavement as she fought to get at the two men. Ernie pulled her onto the driveway. At the gate, he released her collar and she ran, tail high, around to the back of the house. She pranced up the stairs and onto the deck. He followed along the side of the house, past the brick of the chimney and onto the deck.

Lane said, "So, I'll probably be back in a day or two with more questions."

"Not much I can do about that," Nanny said.

"I think we made some progress today," Lane said.

The screen door slid open and Lane looked at Ernie. "You okay, Ernie? You look a little pale."

Ernie opened his mouth and closed it again. He wanted to ask about the men and the pistol. Then he recalled all of the questions in the hospital. Probing questions. "Where exactly did your uncle put his hands? Was there penetration? Did he put his penis in your mouth?" Ernie closed his mouth.

"Bye." Lane stepped past.

Ernie caught the scent of berries in the detective's shampoo and soap.

"See ya girl." The policeman leaned over and scratched Scout's chin. She licked his hand in reply.

Ernie listened to the sound of Lane's shoes as he walked along the side of the house and opened the gate.

"You comin' in?" Nanny said.

"Yes, Nanny." Ernie heard the sarcasm in his voice but it was too late to take it back.

"Don't you be smart with me."

He put his nose against the screen. "I . . . "

Scout barked and ran to the side of the house.

"It's the wop in you. I warned your mother about this."

Ernie felt anger running in his belly.

"I told your mother it'd be like this if she ever had kids. Told her my brother was killed in Italy during the war. He used to write home about the people there. Said the women were whores and the men weren't much better. It's in the blood. Told Beth she'd have nothin' but pain if she married the wop!"

Rage formed the words for Ernie. "If it wasn't for you . . . "

Scout barked again.

The doorbell rang.

"Get the door," Nanny said. "If it wasn't for me, you'd be in jail."

"Better than living with you." He opened the screen and stepped through. Scout followed.

"What'd you say?"

Ernie stepped past, feeling himself balanced on the edge of a precipice. On one side were all of the words he wanted to say. All of the words his grandmother would never forget. On the other side was surrender. The choice his mother had made.

"Goddamn stampede around here," Nanny said, following them to the front door.

Turning away from her, Ernie moved down the hallway. He grabbed the doorknob. Scout was at the window, her nose nudging the curtains aside. Ernie opened the door. Scout growled.

The two men, their shoulders close together, looked like the front line of a geriatric football team. A pair of bellies curved and fell out between suspenders. The bald one wore a blue golf shirt. Round Face still wore his grey jacket over a blue golf shirt.

"We're here to ask some questions about Robert Swatsky," Round Face said.

Ernie felt Scout's nose push between his calves. She barked and squirmed outside. Her teeth were bared. There was a hollow thump as Round Face's square-toed boot met her ribs. She yelped once before collapsing at the boy's feet. "You bastards!" Ernie said and crouched to put his hands on her side. He felt her ribs rise as she struggled to breathe. She whimpered when he found the place where she'd been kicked.

"What are you two doing here?" Nanny said.

Ernie looked over his shoulder at her.

"Friggin' dog came after us!" Round Face said.

Ernie began to straighten up. Fear was replaced by an anger so deep he almost remembered where he'd felt it once before. He crouched, left foot ahead of right, keeping his knees and elbows bent the way he'd been taught. His fists were clenched tight against his ribs.

"Ernie!" Nanny said. "No more of that goddamned karate!"

He took a step forward. The men looked at one another. Round Face moved his right hand inside his jacket.

"Ernie! For Christ's sake, no!"

He took another step.

"Ernie!" Come here!" Nanny gripped the back of his shirt.

Ernie turned to her.

"Stick with Granny, boy," Round Face said.

Nanny reached out and grabbed the muscle running from Ernie's neck to his shoulder. He leaned his head into the pain. She looked at the two men, "You're Bob's buddies."

"We're private investigators." Round Face stuck his right thumb in behind a suspender.

"Bullshit! You're Lester," she said to Round Face then pointed at Baldy, "You're Marvin. I bet the two of you are lookin' for Bob and his money. I remember you tried to put the scare into me when my Judy ran away."

"You're crazy," Lester said before glancing at his brother.

Nanny stepped toward them. "Where's my Judy?"

"How the hell would we know?"

"I swore after you two and Bob messed up my family, I'd never let anyone do that again." She reached into her pocket and pulled out a pack of cigarettes.

"What can you do about it?" Lester's smile revealed a gold crown.

"Ever seen what happens when fire and oxygen mix?" She moved a step closer to them.

They stepped back. "You always were a crazy bitch." Lester put his hands out to push her away.

"Still am." She opened the cigarette package and lifted out a red lighter.

"We're not afraid of you!" Lester said over his shoulder while backing away. "You and your wop grandson!"

"Come close to me or mine again and I'll . . ." she pulled the oxygen tubes over her head, dropped them to the ground, put a smoke between her lips and lit up, " . . . burn the pair of you."

Ernie and Nanny watched as the brothers hurried across the street and opened the doors of the Ford.

"Took me a while to figure out that the reason those two are always trying to scare other people is 'cause they're chicken." She pointed the cigarette at the retreating pair. "When somebody like that is always trying to scare you, it means there's a good chance they're afraid."

"Just like Bob," Ernie said.

"That's right." She put the cigarette to her lips. "I'm gonna make a fresh pot of coffee. Want a cup?"

CHAPTER 3

"I just can't cope with it!" Nanny's voice spit words like a router spit wood.

Beth felt the slick white meat of potato in her palm as she peeled. She thought, Remember that time you almost cut your finger off? So much blood in the sink. Water turning from pink to red. The white skin of the potato painted by blood. What had Mom been saying? "If you run away like your sister, it'll kill me." The doctor said the words the day after Beth's thirteenth birthday. Nanny never forgot them and reminded Beth whenever . . .

"Ernie, his pervert grandfather, the police, and Bob's tough friends. Any more of this'll kill me! Are you listening to me?" Nanny said.

Beth sliced the potato in half, dropped the pair into the pot and watched them sink. "Yes."

"What did I say then?"

"Ernie, his pervert grandfather, the police, and Bob's tough friends. Any more of this'll kill me." Beth wiped the back of her wrist across her forehead. Through her reflection in the window, she watched Ernie picking up Scout's turds in the backyard.

She saw her reflection superimposed around the boy and said, "Middle-aged, recently divorced, living with Mom."

"What'd you say?"

"Nothing." She picked up another potato. The pot began to boil.

"Speak up! I'm deaf you know!" Nanny leaned to pick up her smokes.

Christ, she's gonna blow us up, Beth thought. "It's beautiful out. Why not go outside on the deck?"

"It's my house and I'll do what I damned well please!"

Scout's nose peeked out from under the table. Beth said, "How are you doing, girl?" Scout's nose lifted and she crawled forward.

"I told you, I can't cope anymore!" Nanny said.

"Feeling more like yourself?" Beth said to Scout.

"No! Haven't you been listening?" Nanny stabbed the air with an unlit cigarette.

"I think we should call the police."

"Police couldn't help when they took my Judy away." Nanny took a breath. "Police couldn't help when they broke into the store." Leona lifted a Kleenex out of the box. "Police couldn't help when they slashed my tires." She dabbed at her eyes. "Police couldn't stop the nasty phone calls." Her right hand shook. She reached for the lighter. "Police couldn't help when they turned my Judy against me." The lighter flared.

Feet pounded the deck. "Hey!" Ernie said.

The tags around Scout's neck clinked together. She whined to get outside.

"Do I have to do everything around here?" Nanny leaned and opened the sliding door.

"Don't!" Ernie said.

"It's my house and . . . "

Beth saw the black flash of a rodent's horizontal tail.

"I'll do what . . . " Nanny said.

Scout's nails scattered over the linoleum. She was all teeth and rage.

"Ernie!" Beth said.

A coffee coloured squirrel glared down at them from atop the fireplace ledge.

Scout growled.

"Why'd you let that thing in here?" Nanny said to Ernie.

"You opened the door!" Ernie said.

"Don't get smart with me!"

"That squirrel's been teasing Scout all summer," Ernie stood half inside the room and half out.

"I don't care! Just get that damned thing out of my house!" Nanny said.

Beth saw her son's mouth forming a reply. Fighting with her mother was as inevitable as the coming of winter. The old woman's ensuing resentment thawed slightly faster than a glacier.

"Ernie!" Beth said.

He looked her way, his eyes black with rage.

She motioned with her hand, "Come here, please."

He walked into the kitchen.

Beth took careful aim and tossed the potato. It slapped against the brick just centimetres above the squirrel.

The squirrel sprang.

Scout leapt to intercept. For an instant it looked as if she might close her mouth on the tip of the squirrel's tail.

Scout thumped back to the floor. The rodent landed on the top of Nanny's head then jumped through the opening.

Nanny's mouth formed an O of surprise.

Scout was a tail length behind the squirrel. It leapt off the deck and onto the white table top. The dog jumped onto the table, skidded, and dived over the deck railing.

Ernie heard the air expelled through his mother's nostrils. Beth stepped onto the carpet to pick up the bruised potato.

Nanny patted a rooster tail at the top of her head.

Scout barked and the squirrel chattered.

Nanny coughed.

Ernie took a breath.

Blattt! Nanny farted, leaned forward, and brought her hand to her mouth.

Ernie smiled, Nanny slapped her knee, and the sound of their laughter mixed together.

Beth's mouth formed a straight line. She reached for her mother's inhaler and nitro pills. She had to be ready in case Nanny couldn't breathe when the laughter stopped.

CHAPTER 4

Lane stuffed the tie into the pocket of his grey tweed jacket before opening the gate latch. The sun was warm on his back.

A dog barked.

He closed the gate, inhaling the scents of marigolds, nasturtiums, and wildflowers.

The retriever's tail whipped back and forth swatting hapless insects out of the air.

"Hello Riley!" Lane turned his hips left the instant before the dog could poke its snout into his crotch. Fingers dug into the fur behind the retriever's ear. Riley left a trail of drool across the front of Lane's grey pants.

He walked into the shade at the back of the house.

"The tomatoes are ready, so I figured we'd have a salad," Arthur said, holding a bowl full of diced vegetables in his right hand.

Arthur made eye contact with Lane and winked.

Lane nodded in reply. The wink was their signal that Mrs. Smallway, their neighbour, was eavesdropping. He raised his voice. "Garden seems to be enjoying your attention."

"It'll be ecstatic when you get a few days off, honey." Arthur minced his way around the words.

"We'll have enough vegetables for Mrs. Smallway!" Lane said.

The fence boards creaked.

"Such a lovely woman!" Arthur said.

"We couldn't ask for a better neighbour!" Lane said.

"Oh shut up!" Mrs. Smallway's voice filled the yard.

"We were just talking about you!" Arthur replied.

In reply, they heard leaves and branches rubbing against cloth. Then Mrs. Smallway's screen door closed.

Lane sat down at the table. Arthur set the salad bowl in between a pair of plates.

Lane checked the perimeter of the yard, searching for shadows in the gaps of the fence. He reached out and gripped Arthur's hand.

"Tough day?" Arthur said.

"Oh, it's the Swatsky case. He just disappeared." Lane threw his hands in the air as if releasing a bird, "Poof!"

"Not a trace?" Arthur sat across from him, scooping feta cheese, yellow peppers, green onions, and tomatoes onto his plate. Riley grunted resignedly, realizing he'd be ignored during this conversation.

"Not since he left the mother-in-law's house."

"Tell me more." Arthur spread a paper napkin over his lap.

"This afternoon I talked with the mother-in-law, Ernie's grandmother."

"The boy who was assaulted?"

"That's the one." Lane filled his plate with salad. "Do you want all the details?"

"Like always." Arthur stood, "Just wait a minute." He hurried into the house.

Lane looked at Riley who groaned and closed his eyes. "Don't worry, you'll get your walk." The dog's tail twitched. Lane organized the events in his mind as he stabbed at tomatoes and scooped up the rest. He smiled to himself. People on the force thought he worked alone. None knew the truth. Arthur worked out of their home and was his partner in solving crimes. Arthur's eye for detail was the perfect match for Lane's intuitive gifts. Arthur loved to solve mysteries as long as he didn't have to leave the house.

The screen door closed. Arthur set a bottle of white wine between them.

"Trying to lubricate my memory?"

"Stimulate it." Arthur smiled and poured.

"Ernie left when I arrived to take the dog for a walk."

"Convenient."

"After that, the grandmother started talking," Lane said.

"Tell me everything." Arthur poured wine for both.

"Every detail?" Lane took a sip.

"Yes," Arthur nodded.

"You're sure?" Lane couldn't help teasing.

"Absolutely."

"Pour me more wine."

Between bites and wine, Lane related every detail, each observation and then, "She told me so much, I think she was trying to make it appear she had nothing to hide . . . but . . ."

"She knew more?"

"And was dying to tell."

"Secrets aren't easy for her?" Arthur closed his eyes and appeared to be creating a picture of Leona in his mind.

"No."

Arthur sat back, holding the base of his wine glass atop his belly. "She mentioned Ernie's Italian grandfather?"

"Said he was a pervert. Travels around with a love doll." Lane stretched his lean legs.

"Silicone?"

"Life-sized," Lane said.

"Have you checked with whoever was working at the airport parking lot that morning?"

"It's almost a week since the disappearance. I want to see what happens when I show up on the same day and time."

"Good. Did you talk with the grandfather yet?"

"Think I should?"

"Only lives a block away," Arthur said.

"Okay," Lane said.

"He's retired, right?"

"I assume so."

"Wonder what the grandfather used to do?" Arthur said.

"I should ask, right?"

"Wouldn't hurt."

"Why?"

"Swatsky disappears—remember, he's a mayor, a public figure. Three million dollars go missing. His wife goes missing but there's a record of her boarding the plane. There is, however, no record of Swatsky doing the same. The guy is six foot four, weighs over 140 kilos and no one saw him." Arthur pointed a finger at Lane.

"So?" Lane said.

"Ernie, his grandmother, mother, and grandfather all live close together and one of them was the last to see Swatsky."

"Oh, and there's one other thing," Lane said.

Arthur poured the last of the wine into Lane's glass.

"A couple of years ago, Swatsky was close to being charged with sexual assault. The alleged victim was a six-teen-year-old boy who decided not to lay charges but did end up with enough money to put himself though four years of college in the States."

"Does Ernie know this?"

"I don't know." Lane studied the legs of the wine sliding down the inside of his glass.

"Should he?"

Lane considered the question before answering. "The kid's really shook up about the assault. Don't know if I want to dig too deep. I mean, his parents just split up and now there's the attack by his uncle. The boy's face is bruised up, his nose is stitched and I don't think he's sleeping."

One month later when Arthur and Lane reviewed the case they realized this was where they'd made their mistake.

"Whether or not you talk with the boy, there's one thing for sure." Arthur put his empty wine glass down.

"What's that?"

"Lisa and Loraine are coming over for dinner. Lisa may be able to provide some more background on Swatsky."

CHAPTER 5

"Gonna sit right down and write that bitch a letter," Lester drummed his hands on the steering wheel while they waited for a green light.

"You sure you wanna mess with the old lady?" Marvin said.

"Nobody's afraid of some old bitch hooked up to an oxygen tank. What's Leona gonna do to us? Wheeze?"

"She sounded like she meant it."

The light turned green, diesel smoke puffed from the exhaust of the dump truck in front of them. Lester pulled ahead to turn right off of Crowchild Trail.

"Where we goin'? The motel's the other way," Marvin said.

"Gotta pick up a few things at the Drug Mart." Lester started to whistle then sang, "Gonna sit right down and write that slut a letter."

"What kinda things?"

"They got everything I need for one of my special letters."

"Like what?" Marvin wiped sweat on his pants.

"Latex gloves, black marking pen, tape, envelope, and a dirty magazine." He started to whistle.

Marv shook his head. "I don't like it."

"We'll see how brave she is after losing some sleep. She won't be thinking too straight when I get through with her. Then she'll tell us what we want to know." Lester started to sing as he turned into the parking lot. "Gonna sit right down and write that bitch a letter!"

CHAPTER 6

Red alarm clock numbers stared back at Ernie: 2:37 AM became 2:38. He peeled the comforter off, sat up, and pulled on a pair of socks and sweatpants.

Scout's dog tags rattled. The night light cast thick shadows in the hallway. He stepped over the plastic oxygen line running up the stairs into Nanny's bedroom. The hum of the oxygen machine masked the sound of paws and feet going down the stairs.

Ernie waved his hand in the dark till it touched the wall and found the light switch. Blinking, he spotted the remote control lying on its back among Nanny's pill bottles. He pressed the power button, sat in the easy chair, selected mute and swivelled to face the television.

The screen eased out of black and into colour. He skipped through the menus and found closed-captioning.

He felt Scout's paw on his right forearm and switched the remote to his left. Her cool tongue licked the salt inside his elbow. He scratched along her shoulder.

He tried to recognize the movie. Bullets pitted the wall behind a man ducking into a trash bin.

Scout had her eyes on him.

"You're wondering why I can't sleep."

Her ears perked to capture his words.

"I have nightmares. And I can't stop thinking about the things people say to me."

Scout nudged his thigh with her nose.

"Nanny said, 'If it weren't for me, you'd be in jail.' Now, what's that supposed to mean?"

Scout licked the back of his hand.

"More mind games?" He looked for an answer from Scout. "And Nonno said, 'He's our only grandchild. It's up to us to protect the boy.' He talks to that stupid doll like she's real. Even makes me call her grandmother."

Scout's nose nudged his hand.

He scratched the side of her face. "What the hell do they think I did wrong? Uncle Bob was the one with the knife. Some of the stuff he said I couldn't remember until yesterday. I wish I couldn't remember what Bob said to me. And, I can smell him. That's the worst part."

He touched the scar along the bridge of his nose, "Mom says he's long gone. All the police found was the knife."

Scout growled.

"Uncle Bob may be long gone but he's still hanging around up here," he tapped his head.

The v Channel weather man flashed onto the screen. He wore a green Gumby tie and yellow shirt with half moon sweat stains under the arms. To his right, the moon painted a silver swipe on the river. "Another hot one forecast for tomorrow. It looks like more of the same for the remainder of the week. The only cool place in town is along the river."

Ernie watched the river.

"So, enjoy the warm weather and the rest of the movie."

Something floated behind the weatherman. A log moved lazily. It bobbed once and rolled over to expose an extended limb pointing at the stars. Then it slid back into the darkness.

Ernie felt a shiver start at the base of his spine.

Scout barked and stood up. She barked again and raced for the door. Ernie ran after her. "Stop it, you'll wake everybody up." Ernie flipped the outside light on and peered through the peephole. He got a glimpse of a grey car and red tail lights. He turned the dead bolt and opened the door. Leaning out, he heard the sound of a car's engine racing away. "Back," he said to the dog and closed the door behind them.

"Who's there?" Nanny said.

"There was a car outside and Scout started barking." Ernie stood at the bottom of the stairs.

"What kinda car?"

"Looked like the same one those two guys were driving. You know, Uncle Bob's friends."

CHAPTER 7

"How could I not protect Ernie?" Nonno waved his right hand in the air and changed lanes without looking. There was a scream of brakes. A horn howled. He glanced in the rear-view mirror. The driver behind gave a single finger salute. Nonno returned the favour. "Okay, okay," he said to the doll and placed both hands on the wheel. They turned into the parking lot.

"There's a couple of nice dress stores here," Nonno said. He eased in between a Chevy pickup and Toyota Corolla.

He caught a glimpse of blue in the rear-view mirror, followed by a screech of rubber on pavement. The blue car's front doors swung open. A pair of men stepped out. One wore a black ball cap with a flaming red C and the other wore mirrored sunglasses. The man with the ball cap shook his fist, "Hey, old man, where'd you learn to drive?"

Nonno glanced ahead. There was no place to go. He looked at Nonna, "Just a couple of hotheads."

The men were on either side of the van. "Are you deaf? You cut me off!" said the man with the ball cap. His face was against the glass on Nonno's side.

"Who's the cow in there with you?" Sunglasses peered in the other side.

Nonno felt his anger turn white hot.

"Hey, she's naked!" Ball Cap laughed.

Nonno pushed the door open against Ball Cap. "Son a ma bitch!" Nonno released the seat belt and had his feet on the pavement when Ball Cap pushed back. The door pinned Nonno's shoulder and head. Ball Cap shoved. Ernesto screamed.

"It's a love doll!" Sunglasses laughed.

Ernesto pushed against the door. "Culo!" The pressure on his head and shoulder eased.

"Gimme some help over here!" Ball Cap said.

Ernesto heaved. The van rocked. Ball Cap skidded backwards.

"Hurry!" Ball Cap leaned against the door. "The old bastard's strong!"

A horn blast froze Ball Cap. Ernesto was outside of the van. Sunglasses looked around the parking lot. Heads turned in their direction. "Forget it. He's just a dirty old man."

Nonno kicked out and just missed connecting with Ball Cap's backside. Ball Cap and Sunglasses crawled inside their car and slammed the doors. Nonno leaned his right palm against the van's hood then snatched it away from the heat. Making a fist with his right hand, he raised an obscene salute. The car sped away. The old man eased his bruised hip up against the sun-baked metal of the van. The horn continued to howl. Nonno leaned inside. "Are you okay?" The doll's head was jammed up against the horn. Nonno pushed her upright. In the sudden quiet he said, "Sure, I'm okay." He wiped the sleeve of his shirt across his forehead. "No, I promised you a new dress today."

Nonno rubbed at the pain. "It's just a little bump on the head. Don't worry about those two, they're long gone." He shut his door, moved around to Nonna's side and opened the door. Nonno pulled her arms and let the doll fall over his right shoulder. Her hair brushed against his backside. He locked his right arm behind Nonna's knees. "No, your bum won't get sunburnt." He shut the door. "How else am I gonna pick out the right dress if you don't come along?" Nonno crossed the pavement, stepped up onto the sidewalk and walked through the automatic door. "Don't worry, everybody'll think you're a doll."

Nonno saw a five-year-old boy with chocolate down the front of his white T-shirt. He stuck a thumb behind a loose front tooth and lifted it like a door hinged at the top. "Hi, I'm Randy!"

"Oh, hello," Nonno said then whispered to the doll, "See, I said hello."

Nonno looked from left to right noting the pointing fingers, open mouths and smiles hidden behind palms.

"Don't worry, I'll get a wheelchair." Where the hallways in the mall intersected, a green kiosk sat with a customer service sign under the Lotto 6-49 logo. Nonno got down on one knee to ease Nonna down onto a bench. He carefully crossed one of her legs over the other and turned to the lady at the kiosk. "I need a wheelchair."

The woman smiled back. Her name tag said Marj.

Nonno leaned closer and said, "She's too heavy to carry. Just don't tell her I said so." He smiled.

Marj brushed at a stray hair over her ear. She looked over Nonno's shoulder, then back at him. The furrows in her forehead got deeper.

"Need to buy her some clothes." Nonno said, hoping the woman would understand if only he could explain. "Told her she don't need clothes in the summer but we can't go anyplace without someone making some smart aleck remark."

"This is really unusual." Marj looked to her left and spotted the phone.

"MY WIFE," Nonno said the words slowly and at a traffic stopping volume, "NEEDS SOME CLOTHES."

Marj looked down at the counter top. Nonno read her indecision. They glanced at a sign on the counter: The Customer is Always Right. Both smiled.

Nonno looked over his shoulder, "I wasn't being rude," he said to the doll.

Marj almost broke a nail in her hurry to open the gate. "Your wheelchair is right here, sir."

Nonno said, "Thanks."

"You're welcome, sir." Marj pushed the chair through the open gate and rolled it beside the doll.

"I'll bring it back . . . " Nonno said.

"No problem." Marj held her palms forward while backing away.

Reading the indecision in her eyes, he said, "I know, you're thinking a good husband would have bought her a dress sooner."

"Thank you, mister . . . ?"

"Ernesto, just call me Ernesto."

"Thank you Mr. Ernesto."

"No, it's Ernesto. No Mister," Nonno said.

"Okay, Nomisterernesto."

"Okay, I won't bother the poor woman anymore," he said to the doll. Then he said to Marj, "Thank you."

"You're welcome."

Ernesto lifted Nonna into the chair, bent her knees, and rested her feet on the flat metal footpads.

"Hey Mom, that woman's naked!" The voice was at least twice as big as the child. Ernesto caught a glimpse of her before an arm appeared from inside the western wear store to pull her back. "But Mom!"

Ernesto leaned close to his wife, "I know, I know, she's just a kid. Just like Ernie."

Sunlight knifed through rooftop windows. It formed sharp shadows on the Italian marble floor.

"Remember that holiday in Italy?" Nonno said.

They passed into shadow.

"The sun was strong like today. You had to stay in the shade during the hottest time. Miguel was born nine months later."

In silence, they passed through another patch of sunlight. Red and white sale signs adorned one shop. "Wanna try here?"

They stopped in front of a mannequin who held her arms out to them. She wore a red one-piece bathing suit. "No? You still wanna keep looking?"

Ernesto pushed her past a sports shop, craft shop, and bookstore. Passing a stack of books, he read a cover: *Getting Away with Murder*. Nonno looked away, then said, "I don't think it's an instruction manual. We don't need it. Who's gonna think to dig that deep?"

Nonno leaned forward, listening to the doll. "The other family's gotta big reputation around town. Even if the police do start to dig, they'll have to wait while the lawyers argue. By then, there won't be much to find. Just worry about Leona. Her name shoulda been Big Mouth."

A woman stepped in front of them. She pulled a cell phone from a black leather handbag. Just visible in the V of her white silk blouse was the business end of a gold crucifix.

"Watch out!" Ernesto said.

The woman stopped. For over three seconds she studied the doll. She looked Ernesto in the eye and said, "Pervert!"

Ernesto was caught in the heavy wake of the woman's perfume. "Donna de la notte!"

"What did you say?" the woman said.

Ernesto pushed on to The Sony Store. For an instant he and Nonna were caught on a wide-screen TV. The nipple of one of her breasts caught his eye. For a moment he was drowning. Nonno's feet couldn't reach bottom. Fatigue reached out with cold hands. He took a long breath. Pushing on, he felt the warmth of equilibrium returning.

"She called me a pervert. I called her a hooker." He looked left. The mannequin in a store window had her hands on her hips. She wore a sleeveless cotton dress with blue, red, white, and pink petals.

"You sure?" Nonno turned into the store.

The woman behind the counter might have been twenty-five. She wore the same dress as the mannequin. Red hair hung down both sides of her face.

"We want that dress." The desperation in Ernesto's voice could have easily been mistaken for command.

The clerk's head lifted. Her green eyes focused on the doll. She smiled. "I don't think we ordered any mannequins."

Ernesto said, "This is my wife and she would like to try that dress on."

The clerk stepped back, clutching at the neck of her dress revealing Stephanie on a silver name tag.

"She knows I don't mean *her* dress," Ernesto said to the doll. "Okay, I'll tell her we need a dress to fit you!"

Stephanie looked at the door then appeared to do a mental calculation of her commission. "She looks like a size six or seven. Which would you like to try on first?"

❧

Lane leaned on Ernesto Rapozo's doorbell for the third time. Double-checking the house number, he said, "2412, that's it."

He walked to the side of the house and opened the gate. Shade covered the north side of the yard. The weight of the sun lifted from his shoulders.

At the back of the yard, near the garage, he could see the back of what he assumed was Ernesto's love doll. An accented male voice said, "Don't worry about the police. Ernie'll be fine."

Lane stood out of sight near the edge of the house where raspberry bushes bent low with ripe fruit.

"He doesn't remember what happened," Nonno said.

Lane loosened his tie and felt sweat collecting along his close-cut hairline.

"Don't worry about Leona. She's the one who made me promise. She's got a big mouth but she's Ernie's grandmother. Leona always says she'd lie down and die for her kids. She understands."

Lane reached into his jacket pocket to retrieve his handkerchief. He lifted it to his forehead. The almost imperceptible crack of cartilage made him freeze. No way the old man would hear that, Lane thought.

"They're never gonna . . ." the old man said.

Silence wavered in the heat.

"What do you mean there's somebody here?"

The brim of Ernesto's ball cap appeared from around the corner of the house closely followed by his nose and beach ball belly.

"Hello, I'm Detective Lane." Silently he cursed his inability to stay still.

"Ernesto," the old man said and pointed his pruning shears at Lane's belly.

"Ernie Rapozo's grandfather?"

"Yes. That's me."

"That's a nasty bruise." Lane indicated the swelling on the side of Ernesto's head.

Ernesto reached up with his free hand. He winced as fingertips brushed the bruise. "Trouble at the mall this morning. No police around then."

Lane ignored the implied accusation. "What kind of trouble?"

"Doesn't matter now."

"Mind if I ask you a few questions?" Lane moved out of the shade.

Ernesto looked at the doll. "Okay." He lifted his shoulders in a shrug.

Lane wondered if the old man was talking to him or the doll.

"My wife says you should sit down." Ernesto pointed to an empty lawn chair with the pruning shears.

Lane moved around the other side of the table, pulled out the chair and sat. "Thank you."

"Helen says you should take your jacket off."

Lane slipped the jacket off and hung it on the back of the chair. What's the best way to play this? he thought. If Ernesto thought the woman was real, then he'd have to follow the old man's lead. "Your wife is very considerate."

"Iced tea?" Ernesto said.

"That would be nice."

Lane watched the man's hand as he set the green handled shears down on the table. The old man's palm was as wide as a soup bowl with fingers calloused and nails black with earth. He watched Ernesto move up two steps, open the door, and kick off his shoes before stepping inside.

Lane turned to the doll. Her eyes were blue. Her lips, too red to be real. The shade from a sun hat created a semicircle across the tops of her breasts. The sharp, polished edge of a crease in the dress told him it had been ironed recently. Its floral pattern matched the flowers along the inside of the fence.

The latch on the screen door rattled. "In Italy a grandmother is called Nonna," Ernesto said as he backed out the door with a tray, three full tumblers, and a pitcher of iced tea. He set a tumbler down in front of the doll, another in front of Lane, and sat down between them with his own glass.

Lane lifted the glass in appreciation. He sipped. "Real tea."

"Of course. Nonna likes it that way. Always keep a pitcher in the fridge."

Lane looked at Nonna. For an instant he thought a smile creased the corners of her lips. He turned to the brown of Ernesto's eyes. "Since your grandson was attacked, we've been unable to determine Mr. Swatsky's whereabouts."

Ernesto turned to Nonna and then back to Lane. The old man held onto his silence.

"It's been six days since we found his car at the airport. We've been unable to contact his wife."

"The radio says he stole 3 million," Ernesto said.

"I'm investigating the disappearance."

Ernesto put his glass down and rubbed at his shoulder.

"Hurt the shoulder when you got the bump on the head?" Lane's voice was genuinely sympathetic.

Ernesto turned to Nonna before answering the question. It was a pattern he followed throughout their conversation. "Yes."

"Anyway, since you live so close to your grandson, I thought you might be able to shed some light on the disappearance of Mr. Swatsky."

"Maybe a little." Ernesto took a drink.

"Did you ever meet Mr. Swatsky?"

"Once."

Did his pupils just dilate? Lane felt the sharp shiver of excitement in his belly and fought to keep it out of his voice. Dilating pupils were often the telltale sign of a lying suspect. "When was that?"

"When Miguel, our son, married Beth," Ernesto said.

"Where is Miguel right now?"

"Tunisia. Works for an oil company."

Lane felt himself easing into the flow of the conversation. "Does he see his son very often?"

"Every two months he's back for a week or two."

"Was Miguel in town when Swatsky disappeared?" Lane said.

"Nope. He'll be back soon."

Wait. Be patient, Lane told himself. Set it up carefully, try to make him uneasy, then watch for the reaction. "What was your grandson's condition when you arrived at Leona's house?"

Ernesto's face turned red with anger. He fought to control his voice. "Had a cut on his nose." He closed his eyes and drew his right forefinger across the bridge of his nose. "He was ... How do you say? ... Unconscious. Out cold."

Almost there. Lane was operating almost entirely on intuition. "What was Leona's condition?"

"Not good." Ernesto put his left hand on Nonna's. "She was having trouble catching her breath. And she was worried the boy wouldn't wake up. That Swatsky, what he tried to do to my Ernie!"

Good, he's looking at me. Now's the time, Lane thought. "Do you know where Robert Swatsky is?"

Ernesto looked at the doll, then turned back to face Lane. A slight dilation of the pupils. To Lane it was as significant as the difference between midnight and noon.

"Nope," Ernesto shook his head.

CHAPTER 8

Beth felt the best part of the day settle around her like a prayer. Mom's having a nap and I'm enjoying a cup of tea, she thought. She took a sip and felt the warm gold of Earl Grey wander its way to her toes. They wiggled at her. She pushed her black hair back with her free hand.

She looked up. Ernie used his thumb and forefinger to pick up a green tennis ball. He shook off some of Scout's drool. She jumped at the ball but he held it high. Scout sat, tongue hanging out the side of her mouth. Ernie flicked his wrist. Scout was after the ball before it hit the fence. She jumped. The ball rebounded past her nose and she was frozen; tail pointed here, nose over there.

After the divorce, after Bob's attack, Beth feared she would never hear her son laugh again. But she heard it now. It came from way down inside of him. She ignored the guilty reminder that Ernie had no brother or sister and never would. The postpartum depression following her child's birth had lasted for months. She remembered the fatigue, the hopelessness, forcing herself to eat food that tasted like nothing at all.

"Beth!" Nanny's voice cut through the summer heat.

Beth's shoulders sagged. Responsibility settled in her belly. An anchor holding her on the bank while the river rushed past.

"Beth!"

Beth's motion was well practised. She stood. With a flick of the wrist, the hedge was showered with the remains of the tea. Its amber was suspended, like the dog, like the laughter, like her life.

"What's up, Mom?"

"How long did I sleep?" Nanny sat up with sweaty hair flattened on one side.

Beth looked at the clock on the microwave. "About half an hour."

"The detective. You know, the one called Lane. He went to see Ernesto today," Nanny said.

"I didn't know." Beth sat down in the chair across from her mother. She looked at the coffee table and saw a large brown envelope. "Get some mail today?"

"Oh, that."

"What kind of letter?" Beth was afraid her mother had received more bad news. But what could be worse than emphysema and two heart attacks?

"Nothing to worry about." Nanny tried to light a smoke with shaking hands.

Beth read the fear in her mother's voice. It *was* something to worry about. Without thinking, Beth stood, took the envelope and opened it. "This is disgusting," she said. It was a glossy centerfold of a woman with her legs spread and the fingers of her right hand tangled in pubic hair. FIRST I'M GOING TO KILL THE BOY THEN I'M GOING TO RAPE YOU! was written in big letters across the bottom. Beth shivered. The obscenity fell to the floor. She wanted to wash her hands. "What is this?"

"It's starting all over again." Nanny lit a cigarette.

"Did Bob send this?"

"No, it was Marv and Lester. They've done this before. When Judy ran away I got a letter like this, only it said you were goin' to be raped."

"I'm calling the police."

"Go ahead. Waste your time. They'll tell you there's no way of tracing something like this. There won't be any fingerprints but yours and mine."

The phone rang. Beth reached for it. "Hello." She was surprised by her lack of reaction to the familiar voice. "Hello, Miguel. I'll get Ernie."

It took two steps to reach the kitchen window. "Ernie, it's your Dad. Long distance." Beth moved back into the family room, picked the picture off the floor and slid it into the envelope.

"What does that son of a bitch want?" Nanny said.

The screen door squealed open. Ernie and Scout bounded inside. He reached the phone in three long strides. "Dad?"

"Take your shoes off!" Nanny said.

Beth watched Ernie press the receiver to his right ear and clamp his left palm over the other. "Hi Dad." Ernie listened for at least thirty seconds before saying, "Next week?"

"Shit!" Nanny said.

"What time on Saturday?" Ernie said.

"Don't forget the oxygen," Beth nodded at the plastic lines under her mother's nostrils. She turned to Ernie, saw the colours of the bruise on his cheek and the scar on his nose. Later, when she had the time to think back on this day, she realized this was when she became a different person. When she discovered that anger could make her walk right over top of her fear and grind it into the ground like it was a cigarette butt. How she hated cigarettes!

"Don't tell me what to do in my own house!" Nanny said.

"7:30?" Ernie asked.

"Get me another pack of smokes," Nanny demanded.

Beth was motionless.

"Where? You wanna go where?" Ernie said.

Ordinarily Beth would have been hurt with her son's happiness at hearing from a mostly absent father. And she would have buried that hurt. Not any more, Beth thought.

"Tell him your mother could use more money for support!" Nanny said.

Being caught in the crossfire was familiar territory for Beth. She was sure Ernie would be furious when he got off the phone. Still, she thought, Canadians have a tradition for peacekeeping. Beth held the joke inside and put a hand to her chest.

"Sounds great, Dad!"

"Beth? You gonna let him go?" Nanny said.

"I'll see you at the airport," Ernie said.

"Who's gonna tell Miguel what's happened? It'll end up being the women 'cause the men in this family got no balls!" Nanny said.

"Coglioni," Beth corrected in Italian. "Ernie, take the dog for a walk. I need to talk with your grandmother."

"I just finished throwing the ball," Ernie said.

"Take her for a walk, please," Beth said. "Your grandmother and I have some talking to do."

Ernie was about to argue when the phone rang.

"Who's calling now?" Nanny picked though the clutter atop the coffee table and found a fresh package of cigarettes. "Damned phone."

Scout led and Ernie followed. He grabbed her leash and his shoes.

Nanny stood and shuffled over to the phone. Beth stood, arms crossed under her breasts.

The phone rang twice more before Leona reached it. "Hello? Judy? Where are you?"

"Cayman Islands!" Nanny said. "Where the hell is that?"

Ernie left.

Nanny covered the phone with her palm and said to Beth, "It's Judy." Leona took her hand away from the mouthpiece, "I was just tellin' Beth."

Beth held her hand and wiggled her index finger in front of Leona's face. Nanny's mouth dropped open. She stared at her daughter's hand. Beth grabbed the phone. "Judy? It's Beth."

"Oh, hello Beth. I was just calling to see if you'd heard from Bob," Judy said.

Beth heard ocean waves in the background. "No, we don't know where Bob is. Did you know Bob attacked my son?"

"What are you talking about?" Judy said.

"It's called sexual assault."

"Bob wouldn't do that!" Judy said.

"You haven't faced the truth about Bob for twenty-five years, why do it now? And, since we're on the topic of what Bob's been up to, what do you know about the missing three million dollars?"

"Some money is missing?"

Beth rolled her eyes at the innocent guilt in Judy's voice. "Afraid there might be a tap on this line? Guess that says it all. So, I assume you've got the money and Bob hasn't shown up. Well, that bastard put Ernie in the hospital. You're free and clear with a pile of cash and living on a beach!"

Beth hung up while watching Leona's eyes.

"What the hell'd you hang up for?" Nanny said.

"I'm sick and tired of dancing." Beth sat down in the chair.

"Dancing?"

"Yeah, dancing. Dancing around what happened to Ernie. Dancing around the fact that Judy's gone, Bob's gone and three million's gone. And we're left to deal with the mess. We dance and Judy just walks away."

Nanny lit another cigarette.

"Doesn't it seem odd to you that three million disappears and Judy turns up in the Cayman Islands? I bet it's one of those islands where the bankers don't ask too many questions! And guess what? Judy's at a loss for words when I ask about the money. Ever know Judy to be at a loss for words?" Beth said.

"My Judy wouldn't steal three million dollars!" Nanny said.

"And your Judy never ran away at eighteen after bad-mouthing the family business. She did such a good job we had to sell out and move away!"

Nanny didn't answer.

"It's funny, Judy won't talk about the money and you won't talk about Bob or this letter." She pointed at the envelope. Beth thought for a moment, "Judy phones and asks about Bob, so she doesn't know where he is."

"Don't ask too many questions," Nanny said.

"Then tell me what the hell is going on here!"

"Leave it alone. You don't want to know."

"Not only do I want to know, since my son's involved I have every right to know."

Nanny glared back in silence.

CHAPTER 9

Marvin dabbed at his forehead with a short sleeve. Even though it was after eight and the sun was getting close to falling behind the mountains, a pool of perspiration was gathering in the well where his belly and breasts met. He wondered if the rumours about prisons were true. After what Lester wrote, and what they helped Bob steal, Marv figured it was only a matter of time before he found out about jails first-hand.

The awning out front of Buster's Ice Cream Shoppe provided no shade. A blue neon light winked on: All Elvis. Marvin watched the cars pushing through the midday air on the four lanes of Parkdale Boulevard and thought about his recent fear of enclosed spaces. He'd gone inside, seen the jukebox, walls covered with velvet paintings of Elvis, a row of freezers, and walked back outside. He closed his eyes, listened to the hum of tires.

The door to Buster's opened and Lester was followed out with "A hunk, a hunk, of burnin' love." The door closed. The music died. Lester handed his brother an ice cream, "Double rocky road."

Marvin took the cone and licked its cool chocolate. "I thought he said one."

Les sat down. He leaned back. The wood complained. He eyed his double-decker vanilla, "One what?"

"One million. Newspapers said Bob took 3 million."

"We've been over this." Lester closed his eyes.

"He told us one."

Les licked his ice cream.

"We held the phony meetings, set up the phony deal, made the buys. Three million's gone. It's only a matter of time before the Mounties come lookin' for us." Marv pointed at the road with his ice cream.

Les licked his lips, "That's why we need to find Bob."

"I bet he left the country so we could take the blame." Marvin licked around the cone to get at the melting ice cream.

"Bob said he'd leave our share in a Calgary account. He'd phone us with the number and the branch."

"You still think we can trust him?"

"Remember how Bob used to brag about writing up his father's will to screw his brothers and sisters?" Lester said.

"Yeah," Marv said.

"Bob's always screwin' somebody."

"Like he tired to screw the kid?" Marvin wrapped his mouth around his ice cream.

"Hey, nothin's been proved."

"Wouldn't surprise me," Marvin said.

"Look, we gotta keep our minds on what's at hand."

"Like how much we're gonna get?"

"And how we got somethin' on Bob cause we know about every crooked deal he's pulled over the last thirty years. Besides, we got Leona squirmin'. Just give her a couple of days to get worked up and she'll talk," Lester said.

"Think so?"

"You gotta think positive." Les tapped his temple with a forefinger.

"And if we go back there, the old bag's gonna call the cops."

"Think!" Lester tapped his forefinger against his brother's skull. "You just have to remember."

"Remember what?" Marv said.

"What Bob used to say."

"Well?" Marv felt hopeful for the first time since waking up even though he had no idea what Lester was talking about.

"The kid has a grandfather."

"The crazy one? The one who bought that sex doll?"

"That's the one," Lester said.

"Don't you have one of those in your closet at home?"

"Shut up about that, I told you to forget it, you shithead!"

Marv took a long, thoughtful lick of the ice cream and waited.

"So, we lay off the old bag. She knows us and carries a grudge. But the letter is gonna make her twitchy."

"Like the time we cut the tires on her car when Judy ran away?" Marvin said.

"Stay with me, Marv. That happened a long time ago."

"How did she know it was us anyway?"

"Look!" Lester poked his brother between the eyes with his forefinger, "The crazy old bastard grandfather lives a block away from Leona. I'll bet he knows something."

"So we watch the old man?"

"You got it."

A grey Mercedes drove past and Marvin smiled. "Gonna get me one of those."

"That's more like it. Keep dreamin' about what you're gonna do with your share."

CHAPTER 10

Lane had the passenger and driver's windows rolled down. Might as well enjoy the heat, it doesn't last long, he thought. At eighty kilometres per hour, the wind blowing through the open window clutched at the lapel of his jacket. He looked out along Barlow Trail. It had to be one of the prettiest roadways in the city. Approaching the airport, it was dotted with trees. A bike path ran along the west side. The sun made the pavement appear to be liquid. On his left, an Air Canada jet taxied. He turned onto Airport Road aiming for the parkade at the northeast corner of the terminal. The Lincoln was found at the bottom level, he thought.

He'd guessed it must have been parked sometime after three. The digital clock told him it was 2:30 AM.

He eased right into the bowels of the parkade. Lane watched for an opening in the rows of vehicles. He managed to angle in between a Ford pickup and Nissan sedan. Must be close to where the Lincoln was found, he thought.

The hum of the electric windows was unnaturally loud as he closed them. Lane opened the door and ducked, leery he might scuff his scalp on the concrete. While dropping coins into the meter, he watched to see if anyone was sitting on a nearby patch of grass. People established patterns they didn't think much about but those patterns could help Lane get the answers he needed.

The blast of a horn caused him to look left. A taxi pulled out in front of a bus and the driver of a van had his palm jammed onto the horn. Wheels locked and tires screamed.

Lane felt the ominous collective intake of breath as passersby waited. Lane winced. It seemed inevitable that the vehicles would collide. But the taxi sped away unscathed.

Independent Car Rentals caught his eye. It was under the cover of the car park. He walked toward the parking space where the Lincoln had been found. Checking his notebook, he read, "Swatsky's Lincoln found at 7:00 PM. Tuesday." He looked through the glass front of the rental car agency. A man and woman faced one another behind the counter. The door was propped open with a wooden wedge. The man's hair was cut short. Hers was black and shoulder length.

Lane got close enough to hear the man, "You asked, so I told you."

"You're sure?" she said.

Lane heard lack of conviction in her voice.

The man said, "You wanted to hear the honest truth."

Lane rubbed his top lip to hide a smile.

"Ya, but." The woman shook her head to say no.

"You ask for the truth and when you get it, you don't want it." The man put his hands up to signal surrender.

She said, "Men," and turned to face Lane as he stepped inside the door. "May I help you?"

Lane read her name tag, Tracey, and said, "I'm Detective Lane."

Tracey put her hands on the counter and Lane noted the wedding band on her left hand. She looked left at the man and Lane read his name tag, Graham. "It's about the Lincoln?" Graham started to smile, but stopped at a grin.

Another wedding band, Lane noticed. "If you're talking about the Lincoln belonging to Robert Swatsky, then, yes."

Tracey said, "He's the guy who stole 3 million and tried to rape his nephew, right?"

"He's a suspect in those crimes," Lane said.

Graham snorted to indicate the verdict was already in.

"I'm trying to establish what time the Lincoln arrived and I was hoping you might be able to help," Lane said.

"So many cars pull in and out of here, I've stopped paying much attention," Graham said.

"Were both of you working here last Tuesday?" Lane asked.

Tracey took this one, "He works seven to four and I work three to nine."

"Either of you have any idea when the Lincoln might have arrived?" Lane said. "Mr. Swatsky is an imposing figure."

They looked at each other and as one replied, "Nope."

Lane scanned the office and spotted a long-legged Barbie doll sitting under the fan. The doll's platinum hair shivered in the breeze. "What's the doll for?"

"His idea." Tracey pointed at Graham.

"It's a joke," Graham said.

Lane felt himself at an open door, adrenaline pumping, ready for a leap into a wild, exhilarating sky.

Graham rushed on to explain, "I just got into work, when was it?" He looked at Tracey.

"Last Tuesday."

"That's right. Anyway, this old guy walks past our door. He's carrying this life-sized love doll over his shoulder. And, let me tell you, she was anatomically correct! While he's walking, he's talking to the doll, answering questions, carrying on a conversation."

Lane pulled out his notebook. "Could you describe the man?"

"No, but Graham sure can describe the doll. Wants one of his own now." Tracey said. "Men aren't interested in a real woman. They prefer plastic. He spends his time on the internet." She jerked her thumb in Graham's direction. "Searching for love dolls. The one he likes sells for about $6,000 Canadian. It's made of silicone."

❧

A week ago today, were you at the airport? Lane thought the question through. He considered the tone, about keeping his voice steady before slipping the question in as if it were a comment about flowers in Ernesto Rapozo's garden.

Driving across town usually took forty minutes. At this time of the day it took longer. Tempers tended to get pretty thin in the rush hour heat.

Stopping behind a block-long line of cars at a red light on John Laurie Boulevard, he looked at the driver in the next lane. The black-haired woman had her mouth wide open in song. Lane looked in the back seat. A toddler, with a round red face, tight fists, and mom's black hair, was screaming. The child took a breath. The mother sang on. Lane remembered his family. Old pain surfaced and submerged. Not now, he thought, stay on the job.

At the next set of lights, he turned left then took a right at the Petro-Canada. Lane spotted Scout. Her leash was stretched tight as a guitar string and Ernie leaned back, holding on. Lane was struck by the feeling he might be about to turn the boy's world upside down again.

Maybe I should wait for tomorrow, Lane thought, then thought again. The old man won't be expecting me back so soon. He turned onto Ernesto's street and noted the grey Taurus. Lane was too intent on Ernesto to think much about the two men sitting inside the Ford.

He stopped behind Ernesto's van, opened the door, and pulled the key out of the ignition. Slow down, Lane thought. Think about what you're going to say.

The trees behind the perimeter of hedge hid all but the roof of Ernesto's house. Lane estimated twenty years of growth had gone into creating the barrier. I wonder what it looks like when the leaves fall off? He moved around the car and onto the sidewalk.

Lane felt the branches of the hedge reach out for him. He eased through the opening, turned left and took a deep breath of cooler, shaded air.

The love doll sat at the backyard table. The smoky scent of beef on the barbecue curled itself around him. He realized breakfast had been his last meal.

Lane could see that Nonna's hair had been brushed. She was turned to the right, her arms resting in the chair's arms. He got the feeling she was watching someone across the yard. God, Lane thought, the old man's got me thinking she's real.

Clunk. The barbecue lid closed.

Ernesto held a plate of ribs. Seeing Lane, he said, "We're just having supper."

"I've caught you at a bad time," Lane said.

"Nonna says you should sit down for supper. You must be hungry. There's plenty." Ernesto patted his generous belly and winked, "She doesn't eat much."

Lane spotted a salad bowl on the table.

"It's all outta my garden."

"I . . ." Lane realized he was the one put off balance.

"Sit down, I'll get another plate. Nonna likes the company." Ernesto set the ribs down in front of the doll. "Nonna asks if you're off duty."

"No."

"Water then?"

Lane nodded. This wasn't going as planned. Too late to back away, he thought.

"Sit," Ernesto said.

Lane moved closer to the table.

"Too hot for the jacket." Ernesto said before entering the house.

Lane hung his jacket on the back of the chair. The pistol felt heavier once it was out in the open. He studied the garage with its swaybacked peak, the metal garden shed and the flowers. It feels a lot like home, except, he thought, for the doll. The breeze pushed hair across her eyes. She focused on him. He rubbed his eyes. Must be the heat, he thought.

The screen door screeched open. Ernesto backed out, carrying a tray.

"What do you put on your ribs?" Lane said.

"It's my own recipe. Oil, red wine, oregano, and a touch of freshly-squeezed lemon. I don't usually tell anyone but she says I should be honest with you."

Lane felt an unfamiliar pang of guilt. He'd never run into a case quite like this one and the media would have a field day if they tied Ernesto and the doll to Swatsky's disappearance. I wonder if the old man has Swatsky's money, he thought. Suspicion tugged at him.

"Eat and help yourself to the salad. It's orgasmic."

Lane smiled. The old man was unaware of his faux pas. Lane picked up a rib and tasted the meat.

"She says I eat too much barbecue. Puts the weight on. I say I'm seventy years old and it's time to enjoy this life. She says no sense rushing to the grave and I say she should know!

She says both of us have spent most of our time together in a graveyard! I just dug the holes, haven't spent any time in one yet!"

Lane looked from Ernesto to the doll, feeling as if he were in the middle of a conversation he couldn't quite catch up with.

"He doesn't know?" Ernesto's laughter was cut off at the knees. "I apologize!"

Lane allowed the confusion to show on his face.

"After she died, I got a job at her cemetery."

⁂

Marvin said, "You wanna turn on the air conditioner?"

"Low on gas," Lester said. He kept his eyes on the old man's house. "How long is that cop gonna stay in there?"

"We still got the credit cards."

"Nearly over the limit," Lester said.

"Wonder what the cop's doin'?"

"Don't know."

"How long before we're outta money?" Marvin said.

"Figure we got two, maybe three days."

"What happens then?"

"Got it all worked out," Lester replied.

⁂

Ernesto pulled a rib out of his mouth. "Best job for me. Worked the graveyard shift so I could get Miguel to school. You got kids?"

"No." Not in this province, Lane thought. He felt vulnerable around Ernesto.

"Amazin' what you can do when you got kids. The job gave me time to spend with my wife and Miguel. I like gettin' my hands dirty." Ernesto made a broad sweep with his arm to indicate the garden and flower beds surrounding them.

"You've got a green thumb," Lane said.

"The secret is a little bit of lime." Ernesto looked at Nonna. "She says you must have a question. That's your job." He wiped stubby fingers on a paper napkin.

Lane watched the eyes behind Ernesto's hooked nose. "I was at the airport today." He watched for a reaction. Nonno looked at his wife. Watch me, not her, Lane thought. "I've got a witness who saw an elderly gentleman carrying a woman matching Nonna's description. It was a week ago today."

"We were there. Took a drive to the airport."

"The witness says you got into a taxi."

Ernesto put his hand on his wife's. "We wanted to pretend we were goin' on a trip. Like when we went to Italy. So we took a taxi."

"Do you know where Bob Swatsky is?" Lane said.

"She says disappearing suits him," Ernesto said.

Lane felt so close to the answer it was a sweaty shirt sticking to his skin. "What do you say?"

"After what he did to my grandson, I shoulda killed the son a ma bitch myself!"

"But you didn't?"

Ernesto's said, "No, but I shoulda."

CHAPTER 11

There was a familiar ache in Ernie's elbow.

Scout wheezed but refused to surrender to the pressure of the collar around her neck.

"Heel!" Ernie said. They followed a six-foot fence running along John Laurie Boulevard.

Scout turned, glanced up at him and sat.

Dropping on his knees, he got eye to eye. "Look, when we get to the park I'll take the leash off." Ernie stood, felt the unfamiliar familiarity of a head spin, and shook his head to clear the dizziness. "Shit!"

It took another five minutes of the pair working against the leash until they reached the opening in the chain link fence. Just inside the gate was a sign with the silhouette of a dog in a green circle and the words Off Leash Area printed across the bottom. To the right of the sign sat a garbage can. The combination of heat and its contents filled the nearby air with the earthy scent of, "Shit! Scout! Sit still and I'll take off the leash!"

Upon release, Scout was instantly at full speed. Ernie followed along the pathway; a shallow hollow worn into the prairie grass. It curved through the trees and down a gully.

Ernie heard the chime-like clink of dog tags as Scout scrambled in the half-hop, half-lumbering gait she adopted when running downhill. She disappeared beyond the layers of grass, brush, and trees. She barked twice.

At the sound of the dog's whimpering, Ernie ran ahead

and turned right into an area where the trees opened into ankle-high grass.

Scout was on her back, paws clawing the air.

Red hair fell forward, covering the face of the person scratching Scout's belly. Ernie took in the sandals, black shorts, and white, sleeveless cotton shirt.

"Better watch out," he said.

She stood. He caught a glimpse of cleavage. The recognition in her blue eyes turned frown into a smile.

"She . . . "

Scout peed.

"Ohhh!" She stepped back.

Green was definitely her colour, Ernie decided. "Sorry, Lesley."

She checked her legs and sandals, "No problem, she missed me."

"It's just that she gets so . . . " Ernie said.

"Excited. I remember what she was like as a pup."

"Glad to see you, that's all."

Scout sat as if in apology.

"Has to be the sweetest dog around," Lesley smiled.

The dog raised up on her back legs, and snapped her front teeth on a passing bee.

"She eats bees?"

"And never gets stung," he said.

"How've you been, Ernie? I haven't seen you for at least a month." Both knew what she was asking.

He thought about the answer, went to say something and stopped, afraid it might trigger a flashback.

"Sorry." She reached out to brush her hand against his shoulder. "I shouldn't have asked. It's just, you know, we used to be able to talk to each other."

"I can't remember much and what I can remember . . . "

Lesley took her right hand and pushed fingers through her hair, pulling the red back from her face. "It's so hot and I thought it might be cooler down here in the trees."

Then the words came out of Ernie's mouth in a rush. "I get flashbacks. He put a knife to my nose." He tapped a forefinger over the scar on his nose. "I hit him and we fell." No that's not all of it, he thought. Tell someone all of it! Maybe it'll help.

Her eyes were on him, waiting.

"Onions. He had onions on his breath. Every time I smell them, every time I think of the smell of them, I get a flashback." Ernie could see the blade of the knife. Uncle Bob's threat came back to him. "I'll cut your friggin' nose off and then carve out your heart. Now, on your knees!" Ernie felt his index and middle fingers corkscrewing themselves into a weapon. There was the sound of a zipper being opened. Ernie's right hand struck out. He remembered the feel of that soft, fleshy V at the base of his uncle's throat.

"Ernie?" Lesley said.

Scout barked.

"Ernie!"

He opened his eyes.

Lesley's hand touched the side of his face. Her perfume reminded him of raspberries and summers past.

"What's the matter, Ernie?"

"Flashback," Ernie said.

"What did he do to you?"

"He . . . " How do I tell her? How do I say it? "He was telling me to get to my knees and he was undoing his zipper."

"God!"

"I hit him. We fell and I don't remember anything else till I woke up in the hospital."

"Did they catch him yet?"

He shook his head.

"What does your grandfather know about it?" Lesley said.

"What?"

"The police are there and two guys have been parked in front of my house watching his place for most of the day."

⁂

"Lesley says the police were here. And there were two guys watching your house." They sat in Ernesto's kitchen at the oak table. Lesley sat next to the doll.

Nonno said, "Don't know 'bout a grey car, and neither does Nonna. Asks if you want some iced tea, though."

Ernie looked at Lesley. Then he looked at Scout, who had her chin between her paws and belly cooling on the hardwood floor. "Sure."

Ernie and Lesley sat across from one another as the old man stood. Nonna sat with her hands resting on the table.

Ernie glanced at the photographs in the front room. He'd looked at them countless times; fifteen framed portraits. It was a record of his growing up. He hoped Lesley hadn't noticed one in particular.

She pointed and laughed, "Look at those cheeks!" It was a bare backside photo of him on a white rug with two broad smiles running at right angles.

"Nonna says it's her favourite picture." Nonno slid the pitcher of iced tea to the center of the table. Ernie poured and watched as Lesley carefully set one glass in front of Nonna.

Nonno smiled. "You understand."

"You miss her. I understand that," Lesley said.

Ernie watched the smooth flesh on Lesley's arms and the way the muscles moved when her hand gripped the glass.

"Those guys in the grey car looked like ex-wrestlers or football players," Lesley said.

"Uncle Bob's friends." Ernie looked at his dog.

"The ones who kicked Scout?" Nonno said.

Ernie nodded.

"They still there?" The old man pushed his chair back.

"We already checked," Lesley said. "They're gone."

"What did the police want?" Ernie said.

"Just asking questions." Nonno sat back down.

"About what?" Ernie said.

Lesley pointed at the doll. "Did you see that?"

"What?"

"She blinked," Lesley said.

Nonno said, "She does that when she's mad at me."

"What kinds of questions?" Ernie shook his head. Why can't I have a normal family? he thought.

"Don't ask," Nonno said.

They waited.

Nonno said to Nonna, "But we can't tell him everything." He leaned back in his chair.

Lesley looked at Nonno, then at Ernie.

"Nanny told me if it wasn't for her, I'd be in jail. What did she mean?" Ernie said.

Nonno shrugged. "She's gotta big mouth."

"And you said you have to protect me." Ernie waited but his grandfather said nothing. "From what?"

"Look, your uncle was a son a ma bitch." Nonno hesitated as if inviting disagreement. "Ever since he met your Aunt Judy, he's been trouble for your family."

"I know that."

"He tried to hurt you, said he'd cut off your nose and you defended yourself," Nonno said.

"I know that."

"What more do you need to know?"

"What happened to Bob!?" Ernie said.

Nonno turned his back on the doll and crossed his arms.

"What does she say?" Lesley said and put her hand over her mouth.

Nonno looked at the wall behind Lesley.

"Well, what does she say?" Ernie said.

"I'm not talkin' to her."

"How come?" Lesley said.

"We're arguin'."

"And you won't tell us what she's saying?" Lesley leaned her elbows on the table.

"No." Nonno raised his hands over his head and said to the doll, "Non me' rompere i coglioni!"

Lesley turned to Ernie, "What'd he say?"

"Don't break my balls."

CHAPTER 12

"Get me one of those no-fat cones," Marvin sat on the bench outside of Buster's Ice Cream Shoppe.

"You're kiddin', right?" Les said.

"Nope. Tangerine. Get me tangerine."

"Suppose you're gonna join Weight Watchers too!"

"Maybe," Marvin said.

"You make me sick!" Lester said.

"Hmmmm."

"You get so damned optimistic when life's in the toilet."

Marv hooked his thumbs in his suspenders and smiled at the cool feel of sweaty fabric against cooler wood. He leaned his head to the right and sniffed an armpit. "We gotta go to the cleaners."

"We're nearly outta money. Remember?"

"We got enough for ice cream, right?"

Les reached inside his jacket pocket, made a fist and opened his palm. Four toonies lay there. Three polar bears and one queen's head. "This is just about it."

"Got a good feelin' today. Things are gonna turn around." Marvin interlocked fingers across his belly.

Les opened the door to Buster's and stepped inside. The words of an Elvis tune seeped out, "Return to sender, address unknown, no such number, no such zone."

Marvin looked east. A pair of cars eased around the corner. He focused on the headlights, watching for that electric blue of luxury cars.

There!

A silver car with two blue electric lights. The car rode low. It had the look of solid confidence and pride. A 500 SL Mercedes coupe!

A good omen! Marv smiled.

CHAPTER 13

Lane's radar activated the moment he opened the gate to his back yard. Bees buzzed feverishly around the flowers on either side of the sidewalk. He stepped cautiously to the corner of their home.

Three dirty plates were stacked on the glass-topped table. It was then Lane remembered about the guests they'd invited for dinner.

Beyond the table, Arthur peered over the fence and into Mrs. Smallway's yard. He stood on the rung next to the top of their six foot aluminum ladder. Lisa supported one pair of the ladder's legs and Loraine the other. All three were dressed in shorts and cotton tops.

"You're right," Arthur said. The ladder shifted south and he fell north, clutching for the top of the fence.

Loraine (the Peter Pan look-alike) fell backward onto the grass.

At six feet, Lisa looked almost as strong as she was. She peeled Arthur off the fence, then helped him step around the patch of orange tiger lilies.

Arthur rubbed at his scuffed hands. "You're sure that contraption means she's a swinger?"

Lisa bent and took Loraine's hand. They had been utterly devoted to each other since meeting in Vancouver eight years ago. They made an unlikely couple. Lisa the RCMP officer and Loraine the child psychologist. "That's right," Lisa said. "Got called to a noisy party one night. When we opened the front door, there were half a dozen couples having sex in the front room. The music was so loud, they never heard us knock. One couple was using a swing just like that one. They told us it meant they were swingers."

Lane laughed, remembering Mrs. Smallway's comments about their "unnatural" lifestyle.

"Some detective you are. You don't even know what the next door neighbour is up to and it's right under your nose!" Loraine said. When the laughter died down, she said, "What are you going to do when she has one of her little get togethers? Are you going to call the cops?" More laughter.

Five minutes later, they sat down around the table in the fading light while moths circled the electric bulb above the back door. "We have an early start tomorrow. Do you want to know what I found out about Robert Swatsky?" Lisa said.

Lane put down his cup of tea, "You know where he is?"

"Your job is finding the missing person. They've got me tracking the money and that's where this case gets very interesting."

"How's that?" Arthur said.

Loraine listened closely while rubbing Riley behind the ear.

"So far, we know for certain that Mr. Swatsky diverted two million belonging to the City of Red Deer. He used the money to buy up land around a petro chemical plant east of town. Somehow, he'd got wind of the plant's planned expansion. He got a couple of his partners to buy up the land in specific locations around the plant. Since the company had nowhere else to go, they bought the land at a much higher price," Lisa said.

"Who were the partners?" Lane pulled out a notebook.

"A pair of brothers by the name of Lester and Marvin Klein. Apparently they are long time acquaintances of Mr. Swatsky."

"Who else is in on the three million dollar deal?" Arthur said.

Lisa said, "Actually, I'd estimate the amount is closer to 13 million. I can't prove it yet, but it looks like insiders from the plant, the provincial government, and Red Deer's accounting department were in on the scam."

"How did you get wind of the deal?" Lane said.

"A guy from Red Deer's accounting department walked into our detachment. He said he wasn't sure who was in on the deal and he was pretty scared because he figured someone from the province was in on it. He had a pretty good idea about the amount of money involved. The guy was scared. The Klein boys can be brutal."

"For instance?" Arthur said.

"Lester Klein has been convicted of assault and charged with dangerous use of a firearm. He got off because his brother gave him an alibi." Lisa reached over to pet Riley.

Lane circled 13 million dollars on the page of his notebook. "Any idea where the money is now?"

Lisa said, "It looks like 13.5 million was transferred electronically to a bank in the Cayman Islands."

"Isn't that where Swatsky's wife ended up?" Arthur said.

Lisa said, "Actually, she's his ex-wife. They got divorced a month ago. She made six trips to the Caymans in the last ten months. She also bought a house on a beach for nearly 1.3 million US. The purchase was finalized a week after her divorce with Bob."

"The dates of the divorce and purchase seem pretty convenient," Loraine said.

Lisa nodded, "They might have figured the divorce would be a good way to hang on to the money and the new house if news of the scam got out."

"Judy Swatsky has much to gain if Bob doesn't surface," Lane said.

"Don't forget about Judy's daughter. There is evidence to suggest she's also involved." Lisa said, "What about what you've learned? You know, tit for tat."

Lane explained about Ernesto, the doll, and the airport.

When he was finished, Loraine said, "Seems like everyone has forgotten about the boy. What is his name?"

"Ernie," Arthur said.

Arthur took Riley's leash in hand. Lane's antenna went up.

Loraine said, "It's been my experience that when young people are attacked like that, there can be some pretty nasty emotional and psychological after-effects. Is anybody looking out for the kid? And speaking of psychology, Lane, are you finished talking shop?"

"What's going on?" Lane said.

"You and I are going to talk while Lisa and Arthur take Riley for a walk," Loraine said.

"As a shrink?" Lane said as Arthur and Lisa stood.

"As a friend," Loraine said.

Riley was already at the gate with his tail wagging. Lisa and Arthur followed.

"You planned this," Lane said.

"Arthur's worried. He sees you shutting down emotionally as you get deeper into this case. He thinks it brings old memories to the surface," Loraine said.

"Then he should have asked me himself."

"Would you have listened?

"No."

"Will you listen to me?" Loraine said.

Lane's hand nervously twirled an empty glass on the table.

"A case like this can bring old memories back. Just like Ernie is going to have to face what happened to him, you'll have to deal with what happened to you."

"Lots of people have difficult childhoods," Lane said.

"Often it's a matter of sensitivity and degree." Loraine looked him right in the eye and said, "The sensitivity that makes you successful in your work also makes it harder for you to deal with what you've experienced. You have to deal with it sometime. More often than not, when we reach a certain age we have to face the traumas that have shaped us. Arthur told me about some of the things that happened to you."

"So, what are you saying to me?"

"Listen to Arthur when he says you need help," Loraine said.

Lane forced a smile and thought, Arthur, you bastard.

CHAPTER 14

"How come you're not coming downstairs?" Beth sat a plate of spaghetti on the night table in her mother's bedroom.

Nanny sat in the high-backed oak chair by the window. "See that car there?" She pointed past the T intersection to the road leading to Ernesto's house. She handed binoculars to Beth.

Beth took them and said, "Which one?"

"The grey one."

Beth studied the binoculars. "Weren't these Dad's?"

"Brought 'em back from the war."

Beth lifted the glasses to her eyes. Two men sat side by side in the front seat of a Ford. "Who are they?"

"Marv and Lester. Bob's friends." She spat the names out like they were clots of phlegm.

"How do you know it's them?" Beth said.

"They're the ones who came to the door the other day. They dropped off the letter to scare me off. Saw 'em drive up yesterday and earlier today." Nanny's hand was a river system of veins caressing the back of Beth's blouse. "Didn't think they'd give up. They don't think I'm serious. I knew they'd be back after the dirty letter."

"What do you mean about them not taking you seriously?"

"I told them I'd protect my own."

"We'd better call the police."

"Then what?" Nanny said.

"What do you mean?"

"What are the police gonna do?"

"Chase them off." Beth felt a familiar tightness in the muscles around her ribs. Life was spinning out of control again and she was the same terrified kid whose sister ran away just before her mother fell apart.

"Those two'll just find another way to do what they're gonna do. They did before. Remember?"

"What do you want me to do then?" Beth sat on the edge of the mattress.

"Nothin'."

Beth opened her mouth and stopped, then changed the subject, "It's your birthday tomorrow. We should go out for dinner. Somewhere nice."

"Ernie comin'?"

"I'll ask him." Beth sensed something disheartening in her mother's behaviour. "Let's go somewhere nice."

"Sonny's."

"But."

"Got a two-for-one coupon." Nanny picked up her purse.

"How about trying another restaurant?"

"I like chicken." Nanny opened the purse and pulled out a coupon.

"Lots of other places have chicken."

"It's my birthday." She put the coupon back.

"But . . ." Beth knew she was losing but once she'd stopped swimming with the current it was hard to quit. She realized she liked being a fighter and thought, with a shudder, I'm becoming my mother.

"Wanna cup of tea?"

"Sure," Beth said.

"Me too." The old woman lifted the binoculars. "I warned those two and they didn't listen."

"I still think we should call the police." Beth thought about going downstairs and dialing 911.

"Nope."

"Remember what those two did last time?"

"I'll never forget," Nanny said.

"They spread those rumours around town till Dad had to sell the business and school, it was hell."

"Things are different, now." Nanny looked at her daughter.

"How?"

"I'm not afraid of them anymore."

CHAPTER 15

"What, exactly, is bothering you about the Swatsky case?" Arthur said. He bent to hook fingers around Riley's collar.

Lane had spent most of his day off sorting through the details of the case in his mind. Finally, after a supper of silence, Arthur had insisted they take Riley for a walk.

Lane looked across the prairie grass bearding Nose Hill. Below, in the river valley, the Bankers Hall and Petro-Canada skyscrapers stuck their long noses out of the urban forest. To the west were the newer houses, where the land was mostly stripped of trees and the Rocky Mountains formed a backdrop. Soon, the peaks would be silhouetted by the sun.

Riley galloped away with glowing coat and tail held high.

Lane wore running shoes, shorts, and T-shirt. He felt free of the tiny prison the tie and pistol imposed upon him during work days. He smiled at the simple pleasure of an evening where the air was warm at sunset.

"Something is out of place?" Arthur said.

"It's too much of a coincidence. Ernesto at the airport on the same day Swatsky's car was found."

"What else?" Arthur said.

"He's a great cook."

"So?"

"The old guy's a real charmer. It's hard to imagine him as a killer," Lane said.

Riley barked and headed for deeper grass where only his tail was visible.

"A better cook than me?" Arthur pulled sweaty cotton away from his belly.

"No, but he needs a shrink and you think I need one too."

Arthur ignored the sarcasm, "You like him?"

"Yes and he knows more than he's telling."

"You think he's got something to do with Swatsky's disappearance?" Arthur said.

"Will you let me finish a thought?"

Arthur put his palm over his mouth till only eyes and nose were visible.

"He's so damned nice, and . . . " Lane watched Arthur remove his hand from his mouth.

"And?"

"And innocent."

"Of the crime?" Arthur said.

Lane shrugged and looked to see what Riley was up to. The dog pranced through the shorter grass with his nose low to the ground.

"The old woman called Ernesto a pervert. That hit a nerve?"

"Yes, but that's not the only reason," Lane said.

Arthur waited.

"You know what I'm talking about. He's so lonely he gets himself a doll. He's not hurting anyone. Someone labels him a pervert. Sound familiar?"

Arthur said, "Of course."

"Maybe getting a love doll is not what it appears to be. Maybe its got nothing to do with sex. Maybe it's just about being lonely."

"Maybe it's more," Arthur said.

"You don't understand."

Arthur said, "She's real to him?"

"Sometimes I think she is."

"That's what I mean."

Lane said, "I don't know. You know, after the real Helen died, he said he got a job at the cemetery just so he could be close to her."

"Really," Arthur said.

"Said it was the only way they could be together and he could still take care of their son." Riley barked. Lane turned his head. "Sounds like he's found something."

"The cemetery angle might be worth looking into."

Riley's bark became a series of excited cries.

"What do you mean?" Lane said.

"Which cemetery did he work at?" Arthur said.

"Queen's Park."

"Isn't that on the way to the airport?"

Riley yelped. The men turned. The dog's cry was filled with anger and pain. His tail was tucked between his legs.

"Riley!" Lane ran.

"What's wrong?" Arthur followed.

Arthur tripped and fell.

"Riley!" Lane skidded to a stop.

Arthur arrived seconds later.

Riley had grown a beard; a circle of bristles around his muzzle. A few quills sprouted from the black of his nose.

"Jesus!" Lane went to touch the quills and pulled his hand away. "Porcupine. Where the hell is it?"

"Don't know."

Riley pawed at the quills and yelped.

"We've got to get him to the vet!" Arthur wiped at tears.

Lane reached under Riley's neck with his right arm and tucked his other arm behind the retriever's rear legs.

By the time they reached the Jeep, Lane's arms, back and legs were one solid ache. A mixture of rage and desperation drove him forward.

It took twenty minutes to reach the clinic with Arthur sitting in the back seat holding Riley's head in his lap.

Arthur held open the door. Lane carried the dog inside the vet's office. The receptionist took a quick look and pointed to an open door. Lane found an examination table and eased Riley onto it. He put his hands on the retriever's front paws. "Got to keep you from touching those quills. Only pushes them further in."

"Think he'll be okay?" Arthur said.

"Hope so."

"Let's see what we've got here." The doctor stepped in the back door. She wore a white smock, blue jeans, and close-cut grey hair, and spoke with a southern US accent.

"Riley ran into a porcupine. It was a bit of a shock." Arthur nodded in Lane's direction.

The vet moved in between the men and leaned over the dog. "Hey there Riley." She scratched him behind the ear. In a voice full of good humour she asked, "Is he a biter?"

"No," Lane said.

"Well, Riley ol' boy we'd better get busy. This'll take a while. Rose, I need a tray!"

"Comin' up," the receptionist said.

"How many times did he go after the porcupine?" asked the vet.

"We never saw it," Arthur said.

"If we had, there'd be one less porcupine," Lane said.

The vet said, "Porcupine's don't go lookin' for trouble. Better ask yourself if it was just defending itself."

Lane was about to reply when questions about Riley and Ernie coalesced into one answer and he said, "I'll be damned."

CHAPTER 16

Ernie was caught in the distorted reality of a nightmare.

He blinked.

He remembered the horror of wanting to run but being unable to. He saw the knife's reflection. He felt the steel across the bridge of his nose. Uncle Bob said, "Don't make a sound or I'll cut you!"

He was fully awake and slick with sweat.

"Ernie?"

His door opened. A silhouette in a nightgown.

"Mom?"

"You okay?" Beth stepped inside the room.

He heard the fear in her voice and saw it in the hesitating way she moved.

Scout nudged his hand with a cold, insistent nose.

"I heard a scream," Beth said.

"Nightmare," he said and blinked when she switched on the light.

She said, "You're so pale!"

"It was a nightmare, Mom."

"You scared me. That scream. That bloody scream. This has to be the fourth night in a row."

Ernie shivered.

"Come on." She gestured for him to follow.

"Where?"

"I'll make a cup of tea."

He swung his feet out and onto the floor, keeping the sheet across his lap. "Mom."

"Oh, I'll meet you downstairs, then."

They'd discussed every crisis over a cup of tea. He held the taste of Earl Grey in his mouth, remembering the other times. "Ernie your grandfather has died." "Ernie, your father and I are splitting up." "Ernie, we're moving in with Nanny." Each time they'd sought the warmth of something familiar, something they could share by boiling water.

They sat across from one another at the white plastic table on the deck. Each had a mug in hand and the teapot sat between them. Scout curled like a fox around Ernie's feet. The orange of sunrise was a pale line on the horizon.

"What was the nightmare about?" she said.

"Uncle Bob." Ernie took a sip, then carefully set the cup down. A flashback would shake the burning liquid out of the china.

"What did he do to you?"

"I've already told you everything. Everything I remember!"

"I mean, this time."

"He told me to keep quiet and I screamed. He cut my nose."

Scout scampered to the end of the deck and cocked her head so she could see around the edge of the house. She growled.

There was the sound of metal sliding over metal as someone worked the gate latch.

Ernie felt his heart beat accelerating, his bowels cramping.

"Scout?" a familiar voice whispered.

Ernie forced himself to take a breath.

"Ernesto?" Beth said.

Half of Nonno appeared around the corner of the house. "Helen said you would be up. She said Ernie and me should go golfing."

The old man's hand wiped a thumb under moist eyes.

Goosebumps sprouted along Beth's arms and back. "What's the matter?"

"Nothing," he said. "Can Ernie go golfing? Please?"

⚓

"Ernie, Grab my ankles!" Nonno lay on his belly. The toes of his running shoes stuck into the sloping rough at the edge of the pond.

"What?" Ernie looked left and right down the fairway. The golf course marshal had threatened to kick them out last month. Something about not using the proper etiquette, which really meant Nonno had been swearing. Nonno had said it was impossible to prove he was swearing because the marshal couldn't speak Italian. The two had gotten into an argument. Ernie looked back at the tee and ahead to the green. No other golfers in sight. How did he get himself into these predicaments? At least, he thought, getting up this early meant no one else was around.

"Hurry!"

Ernie took a step toward the edge of the pond where cattails swayed. The soles of Ernie's running shoes slipped on the dew covered grass and he fell. "Shit!" He'd tried to warn his grandfather that the slope to the pond was too steep. He'd told Nonno to forget the ball embedded in the muddy bank. Now the old man had the golf ball but couldn't move backwards on the slick grass.

Ernie crawled forward.

"Sonamabitch!" Nonno tried to put his right hand on the edge of the grass. It quivered with fatigue and slipped back into the pond. "Va . . . " the remainder of the curse was lost as his head went under water.

Ernie scampered the rest of the way.

The old man's calve muscles shivered with the strain.

Ernie reached out, locked his hands around Nonno's ankles and leaned back.

"Whoof!" Nonno took a gulp of air.

The boy grabbed the cuffs of Nonno's pants and pulled. Ernie held onto one cuff with one hand and reached out with the other to dig his fingers into the rough. Ernie pulled, dug and pulled until his right arm cramped. By that time it was easier to pull the old man, who was like a seal being dragged over the ice in an Inuit documentary.

Nonno rolled onto his side and spat a mouthful of muddy water. There was more mud in his nostrils. He smeared the black across his cheek. He opened his hand, a muddy paw, revealing the orange pearl within.

Ernie laughed.

"What's so funny?" Nonno picked mud out of his nose.

Ernie put his hands around his belly. He imagined the old man's nose cutting a furrow in the grass. A plow, with a woman behind, skirts billowing, dropped seeds into the furrow and folded the soil over with her toe. Ernie felt the tears rolling out of the corners of his eyes.

"What you laughin' at?"

Ernie pointed at the shadow trail his grandfather's body had painted in the silver tipped grass.

"I got the ball." Nonno rose to his feet in stages. He looked toward Nonna sitting in the golf cart. "I know the boy needs me."

"Okay." Ernie rolled to his feet.

"I know, you say I've only got a little time left." He stuffed the ball into the pocket of his trousers and bent to wipe his hands on the grass.

"What do you mean?" Ernie looked at his grandfather and then at Nonna. This is nuts, he thought.

Nonno's eyes were deep in their sockets; a pair of brown buttons melted into waxy flesh. He stepped closer and Ernie felt the back of his grandfather's hand on his cheek. The old man embraced him. Ernie caught the ever present scent of wine.

"She says I'm out of time." Nonno nodded in the doll's direction.

"Out of time?" Ernie fought his way out of the old man's arms.

"That is the life." Nonno shrugged.

Ernie looked at the doll. A breeze pushed strands of blond hair into her ever open eyes.

Nonno climbed in behind the steering wheel and patted Nonna's knee. He smiled at her and turned to the boy. "Pick up your club."

Ernie bent and gripped the driver. "How could she know what's going to happen?" He slid the club into the bag at the back of the cart then perched on the rear bumper.

"One more hole and we're finished," Nonno said.

Ernie absorbed the acceleration with his arms and legs. The cart's motor whirred.

Nonno turned right.

"Hey!" Ernie leaned and held on.

Another cart slipped out of the bushes about five metres ahead. Marshal was written in red letters, low down, across the Plexiglas windscreen. The driver wore a white hard hat, white golf shirt, and was holding a cigar. Smoke puffed out the side of his mouth.

Nonno stamped his foot down on the accelerator. "Hold on, Ernie!"

The marshal pulled the cigar out of his mouth. "Stop!"

Ernie's knees absorbed another bump in the fairway. The clubs rattled and bounced. He looked over his left shoulder and saw the marshal turning to follow.

"Hey!" the marshal called.

"We'll skip the last hole!" Nonno said.

"What the hell are you doing?" Ernie said.

Nonno glanced over his shoulder. "Always wanted to do this ever since he called me a stupid wop!" Nonno grinned as he took his left hand off the wheel to shake his fist. The cart veered right. Nonno straightened out and said to Nonna, "I've been waiting a long time to get even!"

Ernie looked over his shoulder as they climbed the fairway to the clubhouse at the ninth hole. The cart gradually lost speed. The marshal was less than six metres behind. "He's catching up to us!"

"What's he gonna do, ban me from golfing for life?" Nonno roared with laughter and looked at Nonna. "Now, Ernie's never gonna forget our last day together. Perfect!"

They skirted the ninth hole and accelerated along the paved path leading to the clubhouse. Nonno hit the brakes.

The marshal pulled up alongside them. The tip of his cigar glowed. He swung his legs out of the cart and stood staring at Ernesto, who walked around the front of his machine. The marshal pulled the cigar from his mouth and said, "Only two golfers to a cart!"

"Grab the clubs, Ernie." Nonno stepped between Nonna and the marshal.

Ernie eased the bags out of their carriers.

"If you wanna golf on this course, you gotta obey the rules!" The marshal pointed his cigar at Ernesto.

Nonno turned his back to the man, lifted the doll over his shoulder. A puff of wind lifted the doll's dress revealing her perfect, naked backside.

"She's a doll!" the marshal said.

Nonno pulled the hem of the dress down over the backs of her knees. "Come on Ernie, we gotta go to the mall. Your grandmother needs underwear."

CHAPTER 17

Lane backed off the Chevrolet's accelerator before making a right into Queen's Park Cemetery. The shade trees on either side of the road took the edge off the morning's heat. He pulled in and parked on the north side of the squat green and white cemetery office.

A grey-brown jackrabbit scooted out from under a parked car.

Closing his car door sounded a little too loud in the quiet. Lane felt the pace of life slow. He looked right at the white Customer Service Centre with a Fresh Cut Flowers sign out front. Next to the sign sat a yellow City of Calgary tractor with a bucket up front and a backhoe behind.

Lane opened the door of the cemetery office. A stone bench squatted to the left of the door. Beyond the counter sat a man wearing a green ball cap. He reminded Lane of a Marlborough man.

"I'm looking for the grave of Helen Rapozo." Lane leaned his elbows on the counter top.

"You know Ernesto?" The man behind the desk stroked his chin.

"Yes."

"Police?" He pulled out a pack of cigarettes.

Lane looked down to check if the butt of his pistol was poking out from under his jacket.

"Saw you drive up." He lifted the peak of his ball cap.

"It's supposed to be unmarked." Lane smiled.

"Police cars have a look. Hard to explain, but they definitely have a look." He flipped open the cigarette pack and pulled out a red plastic lighter. "Name's Ray in case you were wonderin'." Ray's chair creaked as he leaned back.

Lane decided being up front was his only option. "I'm investigating the disappearance of Robert Swatsky."

"And you think he's hiding out here?" Ray raised his arms to form a V.

"Haven't found him any other place." Lane smiled till he felt like he was in a toothpaste commercial.

"One thing's for sure, he's not anywhere close to Helen. There's only one open plot near her. Ernesto reserved that one a long time ago." Ray hesitated for a moment, then added, "What's Ernesto got to do with this?"

"Swatsky is related to Ernesto's grandson."

Ray leaned forward, "And?"

"Look, I can't tell you all the details." Lane lifted his hands as if he were ready to surrender. Getting tough with Ray will get you nowhere, he thought. "I'm just checking out a lead." Lane waited. An unwritten code meant city employees were obliged to help one another out.

"She's in Section D Block 19."

"There are thousands of graves here, how'd you know that one?"

"Helen's special. Just about all of us like Ernesto. He worked here for a long time. He told us all about her. I never met her, yet I knew and liked her."

"Family?"

"I can't expect you to understand," Ray said.

"Try me."

"She died of cancer. Ernesto got a job here a few months after she was buried. A time or two, when he didn't know

I was close by, he'd lean on her gravestone and talk to her."

Lane waited for Ray to fill up the silence.

"He kept flowers on her grave. A fresh batch every week, even in winter. Weeds never got a chance to take root anywhere near her. He still comes back two or three times a week to talk with us and check on her. And we keep an eye on her for him. It's hard for anyone who doesn't know Ernesto to understand." Ray stood up, picked up his cigarettes and lighter, "Come on, I'll show you where she is." Outside, Lane stood and waited while Ray lit a smoke, took a long drag, and stuffed the pack back into his shirt pocket. "You wanna drive or walk?"

"How close is it?"

Ray pointed with the cigarette, "Just down the road and to the right. 'Bout a block away."

They walked the road as it descended into the valley. "It's like an oasis in here," Lane said.

"Good for the soul."

"Anybody else close to Ernesto?" Lane said.

Ray's eyes glanced at the Customer Service Centre. He took another pull of smoke and exhaled out the side of his mouth. It hung in the air behind them. Ray's eyes smiled, "He and Randy were pretty close. You could try him."

"Where would I find Randy?"

"Probably up by the mausoleum."

"Which way?" Lane said.

"Follow this road to the bottom of the hill and up the other side." Ray pointed in the general direction.

Lane pulled the notebook out of his pocket. "What's he look like?"

"Big. Wears a red hard hat. Moves like a jock." Ray's heels clicked against the pavement.

The detective wrote down Randy's name.

"Used to play in the NHL. Every Canadian kid's dream." Ray's words were thick with sarcasm.

Lane waited.

"Hates the NHL but helps coach hockey for little kids."

Intrigued by the apparent paradox in Randy, Lane made a mental note.

"Here she is." Ray pinched the end off his cigarette.

The gravestone was one row back from the pavement. Helen Rapozo 1939–1970 Beloved wife and mother. Carved on the same stone, on the right side was Ernesto Rapozo 1935–. At the foot of the stone, orange and yellow marigolds bloomed in a glass jar.

Ray said, "Got to get back to work. I'll be in the office if you need me."

The click of Ray's boots receded and Lane realized how little the man had told him about Ernesto.

Lane returned to the car. He drove around the grounds, finding the green artillery gun between two grey monuments and taking a tour of the pagodas in the Chinese cemetery. Finally, he arrived at the front of a squat sandstone coloured building with silver framed windows and Queen's Park Mausoleum cut into concrete. Lane parked and walked around the outside of the building. He found a man in the shade, sitting with his back against the wall. A red hard hat and green thermos sat next to him. He sipped from the battered green and silver screw-on cup. Lane sensed the power in the man. His eyes were on Lane from the moment he appeared around the corner.

"Randy?" Lane said.

"That's right." Randy looked beyond Lane as if waiting for someone else.

"I'm Detective Lane. Can I ask you a couple of questions?"

"Nope."

Lane waited.

"I already told the police all I'm gonna tell. Lived through it once. Television. Trial. Questions. The gawking looks on people's faces. All the lies he told to try and get out of it. He's in jail. All I know is he'd better not come near me when he gets out," Randy said.

Lane watched while Randy flicked what was left of the coffee onto the grass. He screwed the cup back on top of the Thermos and stood. Even though Lane was an even six-feet tall, Randy stood a head taller. The detective said, "I'm sorry, I should have explained, it's about Ernesto Rapozo. I was told you and he are friends."

"Ernesto?" Randy said.

"Yes."

"He's okay?"

"Yes," Lane said.

"Then why are you here?" Randy said.

Lane watched as Randy erected a wall. The detective could feel it forming around the other man. "I have a few questions."

"You can ask." Randy said while implying that not much could be expected in the way of answers.

"Was Ernesto here a week ago?"

"He often comes on Tuesday to see his wife." Randy leaned over to pick up his hard hat.

"Was the doll with him?"

Randy brushed off the seat of his pants. "Yes."

"What was Ernesto driving?"

"He owns a red van." Randy stuck his free hand in his pocket. "Look, I gotta get back to work. Some holes need digging. Two funeral parties are set to arrive soon." He walked past Lane and around the corner of the building. The detective stood in the shade, realizing why Ray had sent him to see Randy. Then he checked his notebook and was reminded of Ray's nervous glance at the Customer Service Centre near the entrance to the cemetery.

Within five minutes Lane was inside. He saw bundles of flowers in a cooler and in pots on the floor inside the front door. The smell of fresh cut flowers filled Lane's nostrils.

"Hello?" A man with pruning shears appeared.

Lane detected an Italian accent.

"What kinda flowers you want?" The man pointed at a bucket of carnations.

"I'm not here to buy flowers, I've got some questions to ask. I'm Detective Lane. You are?"

"Tony."

Lane heard none of the wariness he'd picked up from Ray and Randy. He wondered why Ray had not mentioned Tony. Surely Ernesto and Tony would have talked with one another.

"Ask." Tony leaned back on a stool and crossed his arms.

"Do you know Ernesto Rapozo?"

Several creases appeared across Tony's forehead. "Retired almost a year ago."

"You knew him well?"

"He was from the south. I'm from the north. People from the north and south of Italy don't see eye to eye."

"Oh?"

"Ernesto was a big shot like all those guys from the south. Just last week he drove up in a fancy car."

Lane felt an almost electric tingling inside his chest. "What kind of car?"

"Lincoln. A big shot car. Got no idea how come he can afford that on a pension. Had that doll with him too. He's a sick man. Talks to her all the time."

"Was this a week ago Tuesday?"

Tony studied the ceiling. "Maybe. Ernesto usually comes to see his wife on Tuesdays."

"What's your last name, Tony?" Lane reached for his notebook.

"Ruggeri." He spelled it for Lane. "You gonna arrest him?"

"For what?"

"Gotta be a law against having a doll like that."

"I don't think so."

"She's usually naked," Tony said.

Lane smiled and said, "I'll look into it. Thanks, Tony."

"No problem."

When he got close to his car, Lane remembered Randy's words, "He owns a red van." Lane opened the door and sat. He wondered why Randy had mentioned the van at all. He hadn't lied, exactly, but it was beginning to look like he had tried to mislead. Tony mentioned the Lincoln without any prodding. Lane reached into his jacket pocket, pulled out the ignition key, and started the engine.

CHAPTER 18

Lane stared without focusing on the spring green painted on one wall of their living room. The colour made him think of wine.

He found the colour appealing, just as Arthur had said he would. It had been Arthur's idea. Lane had resisted at first, but gave in when it became apparent he had no good reason for disagreeing.

Arthur had a gift for colour and, after the initial period of adjustment, Lane had found he liked the decor. It was kind of like the way he and Arthur had started off almost twenty years ago. After a bit of adjustment, they'd liked the way things worked out.

Freed of jacket, tie, and gun, Lane poured a beer for himself and another for Arthur, who sat hunched over the coffee table. He was reading a photocopied newspaper article.

Lane sipped his beer. "This is the best batch so far."

"Hmmmm." Arthur kept his eyes on the article with the headline "Player Convicts Coach With Videotaped Evidence."

Riley took a deep, long breath to voice his impatience.

"He's mad because we haven't taken him for a walk yet today," Lane said.

"Ummm. He'll get over it just like you'll get over being mad at me. Maybe Riley'll stay away from porcupines."

Lane ignored the gibe and pushed the glass closer to Arthur. He lifted his own beer, glancing at the rising golden bubbles. "Looks good." He took a sip. "Tastes better."

Lane sagged into the couch and waited.

After more than five minutes, Arthur sat back. "Interesting."

"How?"

"Randy worked with Ernesto?"

"I'm not sure for how long but they did work together," Lane said.

"And Randy won't talk?"

"He talks but says very little."

"Like the other guy?" Arthur snapped his fingers in a vain attempt to recall the name.

"Ray."

Arthur pointed at the article, "Randy's been put through the ringer. I remember the media frenzy. His face was on the front page of every newspaper in the country. He accused a coach who'd won the Stanley Cup."

"The coach was convicted."

"So was the trainer."

"Randy was fifteen and sixteen when it happened," Lane said.

"He was a first round draft pick."

"And he ended up working in the cemetery." Lane lifted his glass.

"What's it like?"

"It's a quiet place. A bit of an oasis. It's safe. Peaceful," Lane said.

"So?" Arthur said.

"Randy found a place where he is out of the spotlight."

"To heal?" Arthur said.

"I think so. And I get the feeling he deliberately tried to mislead me." Lane looked through the edge of his glass and it magnified the photograph below the headline. He set the glass down. Pulling the article closer he said, "Look at this."

"What?" Arthur asked.

Lane had his finger on the face of a man who stood behind Randy as they left the courthouse.

"Who's that?"

"Looks like Ernesto Rapozo."

CHAPTER 19

"We'll be in and out in no time. The old man at the front desk will never know we've been there." Les kept both hands on the wheel.

"I don't like it," Marvin said.

"We'll park over by Denny's and walk around the back way, if that makes you feel better." Les could smell the fear on his brother. A mixture of sweat, stale clothing, and something else. Something he couldn't put his finger on. And he hated that feeling because Marv had an uncanny ability to be . . .

"Right. Turn right!"

Les hit the brakes and hauled the Ford over to the right. "Shit!" They came within millimetres of swapping paint with the concrete barrier.

"Cops! There are cops in the lot!" Marv pointed.

Les took a breath. Three blue and white police cruisers were parked side by side near Denny's. "Of course there are cops there! Cops need to eat too!"

Marv was a puddle in the front seat. "Oh man. Oh man." He looked up. "One of 'em's a ghost car."

"What?"

"What's the ghost car doin' there? The traffic cops hang around for coffee. What's the ghost car doin'?"

Behind Denny's, in the parking lot next to their motel, a car sat in front of a no parking sign under the red neon of Vacancy. The car was grey and its black-walled tires completed the nondescript look.

"Cops at our motel. Just down from our door. And look." Marv's voice was a whisper behind a hand.

Les eased past. A guy in a brown tweed sports jacket was talking to the manager. The guy in the jacket was about as wide across the shoulders as one of those rodeo calf ropers. Les looked ahead. He checked their speed. "Sit up. Put your belt on." There was the snap of a metal tongue slipping into its lock. "We're gonna need another car."

"A Mercedes?" Marv asked.

CHAPTER 20

"Don't like that new sign," Nanny pointed at the words over the restaurant door.

Ernie looked between the two women in the front seat. Inside an inverted horseshoe over the double glass doors of Sonny's Family Restaurant were the words Have a cluckin' good time at Sonny's.

"Think they're bein' clever changin' the 'f' to a 'cl.' Gonna give 'em a piece of my mind." Nanny sat in the passenger seat of the Dodge. It was older than Ernie.

They pulled up to the curb, about half a metre from the blue and white handicapped parking sign. Beth turned, smiled at him, then mouthed the words, "Thank you."

Ernie nodded and got out to open his grandmother's door. After setting the oxygen tank on the blue painted pavement, he reached for her hand. It felt more like paper than flesh.

"Shoulda got the chicken delivered." Nanny wheezed while she used the top of the door to pull herself out of the car.

Ernie looked over the white roof at his mother and gave her his "you owe me big time" look. Wonder what Nanny's going to be like once we're inside? he thought.

Beth slammed her door.

"What's the matter? I'm the one who should be slamming doors, it's my birthday after all." Nanny had one hand on the oxygen cart and stepped closer to the curb. "I'm sick and tired of this damned machine."

Ernie closed the car door and gripped her elbow. Carefully avoiding his mother's eyes, he matched his pace to Nanny's. Waiting, baby step, waiting, he shuffled along-side until they had covered the two metres across the blue painted handicapped parking zone and stepped up over the curb.

Beth opened the red and white door then waited for the pair to pass through.

Ernie thought he'd died and gone to hell. "Lesley?"

She held red and white framed menus with "Sonny's" written across the top. Along with a smile, she wore a white blouse and black skirt. "How are you?"

Ernie felt heat on his face, opened his mouth to speak and found he couldn't.

"Table for three?" Lesley said.

Nanny wheezed.

"Please," Beth said.

"Smoking or non?"

"Smoking," Nanny said.

"Non," Beth said.

"Smoking! It's my birthday and I'll goddamn well smoke if I wanna." She turned to Lesley. "And I wanna talk to the manager."

By way of apology, Ernie smiled at Lesley.

"Before or after you sit down?" Lesley continued to smile.

She can't be paid enough, whatever it is, Ernie thought.

"After." Then, "Do you need to see my coupon now?"

"When I take your order." Without looking back, Lesley matched the old woman's pace as they passed the glassed-in display of cheese cake. Then they moved down the aisle between booths where walls were painted pale green and dotted with chickens in cartoon poses. A few smoked Cuban cigars and leaned against hay bales. The table was shaped like a D set inside the U of a bench.

Nanny sat on the red vinyl.

Ernie memorized the gentle poetry of Lesley's walk and wondered if she'd ever look at him after this.

Blatttt! The explosive volume of the eruption turned Nanny's face a brilliant red.

Lesley leaned the top half of her body back so it looked like she could limbo her way out of there.

Beth eased around behind Lesley, sat, and slid till she was under the window.

Ernie followed and sat across from his grandmother. It can't get any worse, he thought.

"I'll get the manager and be back to take your order." Lesley winked at Ernie and left.

Nanny nodded and lifted her hand to press the oxygen tubes further into her nostrils. She lowered her hand and whispered, "It's so embarrassing when I get the gas! I just can't help it."

"Nobody noticed." Beth grabbed a menu.

"Too old," Nanny said to Ernie.

"What?" he said.

"She's too old for you."

"What do you mean?" He picked up a menu wondering if it was big enough to hide behind.

"Don't think you can hide behind that. She was your babysitter." Nanny lifted the tube from her ears, set it in her lap then reached into her purse and pulled out a pack of smokes. "I saw the way you looked at her."

Ernie pretended to study the menu.

Nanny lit, took a pull and blew smoke. It hung between them. She waved at it with her free hand.

"They say the tobacco companies put formaldehyde in cigarettes," Ernie said from behind the menu.

"Can I help you?" A man between twenty-four and twenty-five stood at the end of their booth. He wore a white shirt, black tie, black pants, and a smile.

"You the manager?" Nanny blew smoke. It split into separate clouds along the spine of Ernie's menu.

"Yes ma'am."

"The sign," Nanny said.

The manager answered with a frown that said he didn't understand what she meant.

"The sign over the front door. The one with 'cluckin' in it. Don't think I don't know what you're doin'. Change the 'cl' to an 'f' and you got your answer. Take the sign down." Nanny took another drag.

Ernie looked at the glowing formaldehyde.

"Right away." The manager left.

"I'm gonna check when I leave," Nanny said. She blew smoke into the air over their heads. "Gotta speak up for yourself in this life. After my brother died in the war, my mother kept sayin' she let the government take him away without puttin' up a fight, without sayin' a word. She regretted it till the day she died. I told myself I was always gonna say what's on my mind."

"Are you ready to order?" Lesley held a notepad in her left hand. She smiled at Ernie. He smiled back.

Nanny dug in her purse and pulled out the two-for-one coupon. "Double chicken breast, fries, gravy, ice cream, and coffee."

Lesley slid the coupon to the edge of the table and picked it up. Ernie moved his menu to the left, studied the length of her fingers and the way blue fingernail polish reflected light.

"Chicken salad, please." Beth smiled, hoping a ten dollar

tip would be enough in the way of an apology for Nanny's behaviour.

"To drink?" Lesley said.

"Tea, please," Beth said.

"Ernie?" Lesley said.

All eyes were on him. He glanced left, straight ahead, and then at Lesley. She's got great eyelashes, he thought and said, "Cluckin' burger, please." Realizing his mistake, he opened his mouth, looked across the table and saw the disapproving frown lines forming around his grandmother's lips. "Uhh, chicken burger, please."

Blatt. This time, even Nanny appeared startled by the volume.

Lesley tried to hide her face behind the menus. "To drink?"

"Coke. Big coke." Ernie saw people turning to stare at him. He leaned back against the bench, defeated by his grandmother's gas.

"Okay," Lesley said. Ernie watched her hustle down the aisle and take a hard left to disappear into the kitchen. Her laughter was snuffed out when the door closed behind her.

"Don't tell me no one heard that one!" Nanny said.

"Nope, even the people in the parking lot heard that one," Beth said.

Ernie looked at his mother.

"It's so embarrassing when I get the gas."

"Don't worry, everybody thinks it's me," Ernie said.

Beth smiled at him, then. The kind of smile only a mother can muster to tell her child she'd die for him.

"You think so?" Nanny said.

"I know so." Ernie thought about methane and oxygen and what could happen if his grandmother decided to light another cigarette. He felt the giggles grabbing him by the throat and swallowed hard to hold the laughter in.

"Oh, of course." Nanny butted the smouldering filter tip into the ashtray. "People expect a teenager to do things like that."

"Here you are." Lesley arrived with a tray of drinks.

"Thanks," Beth and Ernie said in harmony.

"No problem," Lesley said.

"We want take out," Nanny said and sipped her coffee.

"But." Beth took a deep breath, and let it out slow.

"It's my birthday and I want takeout."

Ernie took a long pull on his coke.

"Whatever," Beth said.

"Take out?" Lesley sought confirmation.

Blattt!

Lesley's eyes opened wide.

Ernie saw ripples in his grandmother's coffee. The giggles caught hold of him.

Lesley looked at him and covered her laughter with a hand.

"Listen!" Nanny slapped the table top with her cigarette pack. "I'm not feeling well and I wanna eat my," *Blatttt!* "chicken," *Blatt! Blattattatt!* "at home!"

"No problem," Lesley said before she left.

Ernie leaned his head back and roared with laughter.

It took him five minutes to get control of himself and another five minutes to cover the thirty metre journey back to the car. A girl of five or six in a flowered dress, blond pony-tails, and white shoes pointed at Ernie and asked, "Was that you?" Nanny started to chuckle. *Blatt!* The girl ran away saying, "He did it again, Mom!"

"I'll get the order," Beth said. Nanny and Ernie continued out the door.

He was holding her hand and easing her into the front seat of the car when she said, "You know I love you." The words created a silence around them. She kept her eyes on him. "You know it."

"I know it," Ernie said.

"Just because I don't say it very often doesn't mean I don't feel it."

"You've never said it," he said.

"Never said it before? Thought you knew it." She took a hit of oxygen.

"But you say stuff." He leaned an arm on the door and looked at her.

"I thought you knew. I say whatever comes into my mind. Life's too short to hold back," Nanny said.

"But?"

"You know I got a temper. And you know I love you. Always have. Always will."

"I know." Careful of her feet and the oxygen line, he closed her door and climbed in the back seat.

"You drive."

"What?" Ernie said.

"You drive."

He got out, circled the car to get behind the wheel. "I don't have my license, yet."

"What are they gonna do, arrest me?" Nanny said.

"No, but they might arrest me."

"Over my dead body," she said.

CHAPTER 21

Marv blinked. The grey upholstery on the back of the front seat was tinted pink. His stomach growled. Grimacing at the stiff pain in his back, he rolled up his blue windbreaker to serve as a pillow.

He tried to stretch his legs but his feet pushed against the passenger door. Marvin lifted himself onto an elbow, eased both feet to the floor and sat up. They were still parked in between a pair of brand new Lincolns. Dew glistened on all vehicles within his field of vision.

He felt the sun's hand at the back of his neck. "Les?" Marv's mouth was dry and he wished he could brush his teeth.

"Les?" He leaned forward to shake the shoulder of his older brother. Les slapped his hand away. "We smell better in the morning. You notice that? Think the cops'll find us here?"

"We're just another Ford in the lot," Les said.

"What do we do now?"

"Get a cup of coffee and some breakfast, dummy."

"How much you got?" Marv said.

Les reached under the driver's seat and fished out a thirty-five millimetre film container he used to store toonies. He poured the coins into his left palm and counted. "Fifteen."

"Bucks?" Marv's belly felt emptier.

"Toonies. Thirty bucks."

"Tim Horton's?"

"Sure. Last night, I spotted one just down the road." Les sat up.

"Then what?"

"We need another car. Cops'll be looking for this one." Les picked sleep from the corners of his eyes.

"Where we gonna get one?"

"Strip mall or one of those health clubs. Wait till someone ducks inside and leaves the car running."

Marv felt better when they had a plan. "Then we'll pay the old man a visit?"

"And it won't be kidnapping," Lester said.

"What do you mean?"

"I'll explain after we have a coffee."

❖

"Mom, I'm late for work. You wake me up at five to look for lighter fluid. You don't use lighter fluid anymore. I'm sure we threw it out after Dad died," Beth said.

"It's gotta be here somewhere," Nanny said. The nightie she wore had been washed so many times that her body was outlined in shadow. She moved across the family room carpet to the garage door. Fluorescent tubes flickered inside the garage creating a soft, eerie light. Glass jars were scattered inside the green recycling box next to the stairs. She looked at the jars and said, "That'll do the trick."

"What?" Beth leaned against the wall.

"It's okay." Nanny closed the door and turned the lights off. She reached for her daughter, and put both arms around Beth's waist. "I love you."

"What?" Beth pulled away from the dusty scent of smoke and perfume, yet remained close enough to keep both arms around her mother's shoulders.

"You heard me."

"Mom. What's the matter?" Beth felt a cold fist inside of her. For an instant she thought she might be sick.

"Can't I just say it without you making a fuss?" Nanny moved back into the family room.

"But . . ." Beth was framed in the doorway.

"I thought you knew." Nanny sat and opened her smokes. She lifted the oxygen tube off her face and dropped it at her feet.

"I do know. It's just . . ."

"Spit it out girl," Nanny flicked the lighter's wheel and flame lit the end of her cigarette.

"You don't say it very often."

"There. It's better when you say what's on your mind." Nanny took a drag and closed her eyes, "You're late for work."

"We need to talk," Beth said.

"When you get home."

Beth opened her mouth, closed it, looked at her watch, "Shit! I'm late."

Nanny waited till the door closed behind Beth. The old woman lifted the TV remote. The screen eased out of black. Coffee cup in one hand and cigarette in the other, she waited until the commercials were finished.

She reached down to put the clear plastic of the oxygen tube under her nose and over her ears. She stood and shuffled across the carpet to the garage door. Flipping on the light switch with her left, she opened the door with her right hand. She wheezed down two steps where the cool of concrete met the soles of her feet. Sitting on the steps, she picked through the glass jars until she found one with a matching lid. "Small enough to fit in my purse," she said. Back inside, Nanny headed for the sliding glass door, opened it and stepped out onto the deck. The sun licked the dew off the wood. Reaching back, she pulled the oxygen line but it was stretched as far as it could go. She took short gasping breaths. It was all her scarred lungs would allow. Her gaze measured the pathway to the shed where they kept the lawn mower and gasoline.

"You've gone to the shed a thousand times before. One more time won't kill you." Lifting the tube over her head, she looped it over the deck railing and stepped down to the paving stones. She stepped onto the grass and smiled. "Move slow." Wheezing, and holding the jar between her breasts, she reached the shed. The metal door stuck at first, but she managed to shake it open. Gasoline, grease, and grass clippings came together to create a communal scent rich with summer memories. Nanny bent to twist the black plastic cap off the red can of gasoline. "All I need is a jarful."

Lane wondered what had been done to beef up security after someone mailed the chief a letter bomb. He couldn't tell if anything had been changed, but then he'd never been to see the Chief of Police before. He nodded at Harper who sat behind a desk in the outer office. The officer nodded in return. Harper was in his late twenties, had thick black hair and an equally thick mustache. He was still built like someone who played on the front line of a CFL team, Lane noted. For a moment, he recalled their first meeting and wondered if Harper was thinking the same thing. Lane sat in one of the upholstered chairs. He took in the room. It was about as plain as an office could get.

Lane wondered again about the call he'd received ten minutes before leaving home for work. "Can you meet with the chief at 8:15?" Lane realized now it had to have been

Harper making the call. The last time they'd talked had been nearly five years ago when Harper had only been on the force for one year. Recently, Lane had heard other officers make cracks about a gun-shy cop looking after the chief.

Lane picked through the magazines to his left. *Time*, *Maclean's* and *Report on Business*. He started with *Maclean's*.

Another officer stepped into the outer office. His blond hair was cut to a length of no more and no less than two millimeters. His boots were polished till they looked like black plastic. "Chief wants to see me." He pointed at his chest, "Stockwell."

"Take a seat." Harper pointed at the chair to the left of Lane.

The officer turned, spotted Lane, hesitated for an instant and sat two chairs over.

Lane noted the hesitation and ignored it. It was old news. People like that can't bother me anymore, he thought. He flipped through *Maclean's* and glanced over the top of the magazine to study Harper. He still looks fit, Lane thought. He looks much better than when he was being loaded into the ambulance.

"Lane, chief's ready to see you." Harper hitched his thumb in the direction of the door on the right.

Lane stood, careful not to show any anxiety, and buttoned his grey sports jacket. He opened the door and stepped inside.

"That who I think it was?" Stockwell said.

"Depends on who you think it was." Harper squinted at the computer screen, clicked the mouse and frowned.

"Detective Lane."

"That's him," Harper said.

"Glad I don't have a partner like that. If you know what I mean." Stockwell brushed a white fleck off the breast pocket of his jump suit.

"Like what?" Harper stared at the other officer.

"You know." Stockwell crossed his right leg over his left, raised his right hand and bent it at the wrist.

Swivelling his chair 180 degrees, Harper stood. He moved over to the chair Lane had left and lifted his left shoe onto the cushion. Then Harper pulled up the left leg of his trousers. In the meat of his calf, about two thirds of the way to his knee, there was a round scar. "It's more of a mess where it came out the other side. My partner and I answered the call. A domestic dispute. When I rang the doorbell, the guy on the inside blasted a hole through the door. I remember looking down and there was smoke coming out of my leg. At first there was no pain. I just fell over." Harper released the fabric and shook his foot. The hem dropped to the top of his shoe.

Stockwell yawned.

"My partner ran for the unit to call it in. Then the pain hit. My partner stayed with the unit. I remember watching the blood rolling off the top step and down to the next."

"What's this got to do with anything?" Stockwell sat with his knees spread wide.

"It's got nothing to do with you but something to do with Lane. He was the next officer on the scene. Saw me lying there and he walked up the sidewalk with his hands locked behind his neck. I remember Lane's eyes. He was taking it all in. The guy with the hunting rifle opened the front door and yelled through the screen. Lane said, and I'll never forget this, 'How do you get those roses to grow? I never had much luck with roses.' "

"You're kidding, right?" Stockwell sat up.

"Then he says, 'I'm going to put some pressure on the wound to try and stop the bleeding.' He moved up to me and put one hand on my femoral artery and the other over the hole in my leg. He kept on talking to this guy about gardening. You know, asking questions about soil, fertilizer, and watering. I started yelling at Lane to get his hands off me. Told him he was a pervert and the whole force knew it. He just ignored me and kept the pressure on the wound. Asked the guy who shot me if he had a towel. The guy handed one out the door. Lane wrapped it around my leg and then went back to applying pressure. The shooter started to talk about how he never meant to hurt me, just wanted to warn me off. All this time I'm still screaming at Lane to get his hands off me, so Lane asks the shooter to help put pressure on the wound. And I'll be damned if the guy doesn't lean the rifle up against the wall and come out to hold his hand on my calf. Lane pulls off his tie with his free hand and gets the shooter to help him wrap it around the towel. I wake up the next day and a doctor tells me I almost bled to death. He told me whoever gave me first aid probably saved my life."

"So you're saying Lane's a little light in the loafers but he's a good cop," Stockwell said.

"No." Harper backed away. "I'm saying I was an asshole then and you're an asshole now."

༈

"Arthur? You awake?" Lane said. He looked through his reflection in the coffee shop window. A bicycle courier tore down the center of the street. A middle-aged man in a grey business suit carried a laptop and dialed a cell phone. A man in a green ski jacket and jeans followed in sock feet. He carried his boots over his shoulder. A shoebox-sized leatherette case was in his right hand. Lane thought about the street people. They were mostly men in their thirties and forties. He remembered his mother bringing him downtown on the bus when he was a kid. He couldn't remember it being like this.

"It's five to nine. I'm never awake before a cup of coffee," Arthur said.

"The chief talked to me this morning," Lane said.

"The chief? You said, the chief?"

"Yes, and I have a new partner," Lane said.

"A what?"

"A partner. The chief said it was time for me to stop working alone. She said I had a better record of arrests than anyone else in the department and didn't want to lose all that expertise. She asked how I did it."

"And you told her?" Arthur said.

"She asked. Nobody else ever did." Lane began to realize how much of a risk he'd taken.

"I can't believe it."

"I always said, if anyone ever asks, I'll tell. She asked, I told."

"What did she say?" Arthur said.

"Fascinating."

"Don't play games. What did she say?"

"Fascinating. That's all she said. Fascinating." Lane recalled the smile on her face.

"You're kidding me," Arthur said.

"Not at all. She's got a sense of humour. That brings us to the best part."

"It gets better?"

Lane wished he could see Arthur's face. "Guess who's coming to dinner?"

"Get to the point if you want me to make supper again!"

Lane said, "Apparently, he specifically asked to be teamed up with me." There was thirty seconds of stunned silence after Lane told Arthur the name of his new partner.

Ernie rolled over. Sleep had opened the door to another nightmare. The knife's blade appeared under his eyes. His nose filled with the stink of onions on Uncle Bob's breath.

"Get the phone!" Nanny said.

The phone rang again. Ernie rolled and planted his feet on the carpet. He stood. The phone rang.

"Ernie!"

"Why can't you get it yourself?" He took four stumbling steps before mind and body began to work together.

"Get the damned phone!"

Ernie picked up the phone and leaned right to look into his grandmother's room. She sat at the chair in front of the window overlooking the street. Cigarette smoke coiled its lazy tongue along the ceiling. A pair of field glasses were propped up, balanced near her left hand.

"HELLO?" The voice on the phone was a nail through the ear drum.

Ernie held the phone at arm's length.

"HELLO?"

Ernie felt knots developing in his neck muscles. No, it's not a nightmare, I'm awake, he thought.

"LISA! IT'S ME, LISA! WHO'S THERE?"

"Who is it?" Nanny said.

"WHO'S THERE?" Lisa said.

Ernie turned the receiver upside down and spoke into the mouthpiece, "Me."

"WHERE'S MY FATHER?"

"Oh, her," Nanny said.

Ernie put his hand over the phone, leaned and said,

"How'd you know?"

"Even a deaf person complains when she's around. A screamer from the get go." Nanny stubbed a filter tip into a mountain of butts.

"ANSWER ME!"

Ernie brought the upside down phone closer, "Don't know where he is."

"LIAR! WHERE THE HELL IS HE?"

Ernie closed his eyes and visualized his twenty-year-old cousin, Lisa. She had ordered him around like a slave for as long as he could remember.

He pressed the receiver against his thigh and said to Nanny, "You wanna talk to her?"

"What for? She doesn't listen to anyone but herself." Nanny sipped coffee.

Ernie held the receiver half a metre from his face.

"WHERE ... THE ... HELL ... IS ... MY ... FATHER?"

"If you hang up, she'll only call back," Nanny said.

"ANSWER THE FUCKING QUESTION."

Ernie put the phone to his lips. "You tell me."

"ERNIE! YOU LET ME TALK TO MY GRAND-MOTHER RIGHT NOW!"

Ernie stood in the doorway. Nanny turned to face him and shook her head.

"She won't come to the phone." He realized his mistake too late.

"WHAT DO YOU MEAN, WON'T?"

Ernie sagged cross-legged to the carpet. First the nightmare about Uncle Bob and now the living nightmare of Bob's daughter. "I'll talk if you stop yelling."

"I'M NOT YELLING!"

"Nobody knows where he is."

"SOMEBODY HAS TO KNOW."

"The police are looking for him. I don't know where he is. They found his car at the airport. That's all I know."

"BULLSHIT!"

"The bastard put a knife to my face, I ended up in the hospital and I don't care where he is!"

"LIAR!"

Ernie slapped the receiver onto its cradle while realizing Lisa was right about one thing. He wanted to know where Bob was, and if he was coming back with another knife.

The phone rang ten times.

"Ignore it. Go and take a shower," Nanny said.

Ernie locked the bathroom door. He showered till the water turned cold. He shut it off and listened. Nothing. Relief and a thick towel warmed him as he wiped himself dry. He slipped into black T-shirt and jeans.

"She stopped callin'," Nanny said.

Ernie waited.

The phone rang.

He hesitated.

It rang again.

He picked it up and held it away from his ear.

"Hello?"

"Dad?"

"Hi. Ern, I'm on my way home. Write down my flight number. Air Canada 597 out of Toronto. I get in at 18:15. They changed the time."

"Got it." Ernie wrote it all down on a scrap of paper.

"How's Nonno?"

"Okay. Took me golfing." Ernie thought about what his grandfather had said about running out of time.

"Still taking the doll everywhere he goes?" Miguel asked.

"Yep, but he did get her a dress."

"Good. You okay?"

"Yep." Ernie lied. Dad didn't deal with other people's problems, he thought. Maybe that's why he took a job halfway around the world.

"Good, see you tomorrow." Miguel hung up.

"Who was that?" Nanny said.

"My Dad." Ernie prepared himself for the inevitable sarcastic comment.

"Good, you need your father around."

Ernie cocked his head to the right and looked carefully at his grandmother.

Nanny didn't turn. Ernie saw his reflection next to hers in the window.

She said, "What are you staring at?"

"You okay?"

"Don't you worry, Ernie, everything is gonna be fine." Nanny waved her hand once as if to dismiss him.

❧

Lane decided to arrive through the back entrance of Queen's Park Cemetery. Evergreens lined up like dark green angels on either side of the narrow, paved roadway. Their scent seeped inside the car.

Ahead, Randy walked alongside the road in his red hard hat, khaki shirt, and pants. A gas-powered Weed Eater was balanced in his right hand.

Lane coasted up beside, "Got a minute?"

Randy's smile faded as he turned. His lips formed a straight line and his eyes adopted a blank expression. Lane wondered if he'd see the person behind the mask. Randy stopped to face the policeman. Lane took extra care as he stopped and shut off the engine. He heard bird song.

Randy held the weed trimmer balanced like a spear, "You hear it too."

Lane stood straight, closed his eyes and leaned till his back formed a gentle curve. "Yes."

"People make too much noise to listen to the music birds make."

"I've got a couple of questions." Lane felt caught off guard by the apparent sensitivity of a man who seemed so guarded.

"Yep." Randy shifted the weed trimmer around to the front of his body.

"A witness says Ernesto drove a Lincoln here the morning Swatsky disappeared."

Randy shrugged.

"Can you confirm that Ernesto drove a Lincoln to this cemetery the morning Robert Swatsky disappeared?"

Randy's eyes studied Lane.

Lane said, "Can you ... " Then he remembered their last meeting when Randy had answered a similar question with, "He owns a red van." Randy is not a liar, Lane thought. His silence is as good as an admission. "You don't lie, do you?"

Randy continued to watch the detective. At first he gave no indication of having heard a word, then he said, "Look, this thing is heavy." Randy hefted the trimmer to accentuate his point. "Let's go sit in the shade."

They walked to the north side of the mausoleum. Randy set the trimmer down in the shade, next to the wall. He removed his hard hat. Randy sat down, crossed his legs and leaned against the cool of the concrete.

Lane sat against the wall, about a metre from Randy.

"When you've been put on the stand, told to tell the truth and been accused over and over again of lying, lies don't come easily. Hanging onto the truth was all that I had left at one time. Then I came to realize it's all we ever have." Randy stared north to the trees and the clear sky above. A passenger jet climbed to gain altitude before crossing the Rocky Mountains.

"Amazing," Lane said.

"What?"

"That's the longest answer you've given me so far."

"Maybe that's because I figure you recognize the significance of truth," Randy said.

"How come you never played hockey again?"

"That's a long story."

Lane decided to let the conversation take them where it would. Randy wasn't about to be forced or intimidated and this way they might end up where they needed to go. "I've got time."

Randy nodded and smiled. "When I first went to the police about the assaults, I was nineteen and drunk. That was the end of my hockey career."

"But you were a top draft pick."

"Number one when I was eighteen. Drank the signing bonus and rolled a brand new Corvette into a ditch. Walked away with a few bruises."

"I'm not sure I get what you mean about it being the end of your career," Lane said.

"By the time I went to the police, the coach had won two Stanley Cups with a Canadian team. People were talking about Canadians taking back their game. You remember?"

Lane nodded.

"Lots of people think I put an end to that because I couldn't keep my mouth shut."

Lane waited.

"Pro sports doesn't like rookies who open up a closet full of dirty laundry. Ex-teammates, roommates, and coaches lined up to try and convince me to keep quiet for the good of the game. The owner and a couple of broadcasters backed the coach. Lots was written and said about me and how I was a drunk looking to make a name for myself because I didn't have the heart to play with the pros. There were also some vague references about me trying to hide my sexual preferences." Randy looked at Lane to see if he had any questions. "Then the video turned up. The tape caught him threatening to end my career if I didn't do what he wanted and he made it very clear what he wanted. I won in court but it made a lot of people look bad."

"So you ended up here?"

"Bounced around a bit first. Drank for another year. Came here about five years ago," Randy said.

"Where does Ernesto fit in?" Lane said.

"He used to bring little Ernie to my hockey games. He was my number one fan. Even went to some of the trial. Ernesto got me the job here." Randy shifted his body to look directly at Lane, "My face was in every newspaper, on every television. I became totally isolated. I couldn't even go to the grocery store because people would look at the cover of some newspaper or magazine, see my face and turn their backs. You wouldn't believe some of the reactions."

Oh, yes I would, thought Lane. He tried not to feel compassion for Randy but it was impossible.

"Anyway, I ended up here. Ernesto put me back together. He used to say, 'That is the life.' And he'd tell me how he'd watched his wife die of cancer. How he could do nothing to save her. How he felt so helpless. How he felt he'd let her down in some way. He learned that life just does that some-times and there's really no reason for it. Ernesto used to remind me, 'You told the truth. Sometimes the truth gets you in the most trouble but you have to hang onto it or it slips away and you've got nothing.' I don't know what I would have done without him. Some of the guys around here would have nothing to do with me at first, but Ernesto had a way of bringing everyone around. Except of course for Tony. There is some old-country feud between them. I assume that's why you're here."

Lane was caught off guard again. He'd made it a rule never to underestimate the people he interviewed and he'd under-estimated this one.

"You don't like to lie either. I'll take your silence as a yes. Don't feel bad. Most people believe in the dumb jock stereo-type whether they realize it or not."

Lane shook his head, realizing Randy had outfoxed him.

"I was fifteen when it all started. At twenty I was still fifteen up here." Randy tapped the side of his head with a finger. "When the abuse started to happen, I turned inward. Blamed myself. Thought there was something wrong with me. Got really self-destructive. Having that happen and then being in the spotlight for over a year, man that does some weird things to the psyche. Emotional and psychological pain is the worst. Take my word for it, I know."

Lane nodded unconsciously and caught himself too late. Randy had taken complete charge of the conversation. It's as if he sees right through me and I'm supposed to see through him, Lane thought.

"Swatsky's story has all the ingredients the public seems to love. There's corruption in politics with violence and attempted rape thrown in. This story will be everywhere if

Swatsky ever turns up. Right now, the attack on Ernie isn't a big story. But if Swatsky turns up, all sorts of conflicting news angles will be out there. And who'll be right in the middle of it?"

"Ernie." Lane felt the weight of choice on his shoulders. The choice, he'd been told, was up to the courts and not up to him.

"You're a smart man. And Ernesto says you're a good man. So, that's why I've explained all of this to you. For a long time I didn't trust anyone. Somehow, I think I can trust you."

"It's up to me to find out what happened," Lane said.

"This time it's a little more complicated than that. By the time the media is through with a story like this, almost no one will know the truth and the victim will be a basket case. One newspaper reporter explained it all to me. He said, 'Look, your story has a life of its own. You're a number one draft pick. Your coach won the Stanley Cup twice and what he did or didn't do to you is unimportant. It's the way people can't get enough of the story that's important.' And then he said, 'Don't take all the attention personally, kid.' How could any thinking human being say something that goddamned stupid?" Randy stood and put on his hard hat.

And you haven't really told me anything while telling me everything, Lane thought. "Have you got a home number I can reach you at?"

"241-1786. Need to write it down?"

"I'll remember." Lane smiled, stood, and slipped an arm into his jacket.

"I've got a question," Randy said.

"Okay."

"How come, after you saved that cop's life, you never got any recognition?"

"How did you know about that?" Lane concentrated on adjusting the lapels of his jacket to hide his surprise.

"It's amazing what you can find out if you have a library card."

"It's a long story." Lane looked straight back at Randy.

"I thought so." Randy picked up the weed trimmer and moved back to the roadway. "Time to get back to work." He put earplugs in. Then, with one pull, the trimmer's gas engine started.

"Never ignore the obvious," Lane said and made for the Chev. He had another stop to make.

Lane parallel parked across the street from a brown five storey office building. This side of the street was lined with mature trees and two storey homes. It was just off Fourth Street where trendy coffee shops and restaurants had revitalized the neighbourhood. He realized Randy hadn't given him any specifics but he'd given him the answer. Lane had to admit the jock was a couple of steps ahead of him. And Randy knew Lane was close to the truth. He sized me up and went straight to the heart of it all, Lane thought. This case is all about heart.

He walked into the five storey building, past the main floor pharmacy, right past the lab and up the stairway to the third floor. Halfway down the carpeted hallway, he pushed open a beige metal door with the sign Dr. Wallace and Dr. Keeler Family Practice.

The receptionist was on his left, behind a metre-high wall of plastic and glass. She lifted her head, frowned and said, "Oh, it's you."

The tone of her voice told him he'd come at a bad time. Lane looked right to see at least ten people sitting in the waiting room.

"To see Dr. Keeler?" The receptionist tapped the side of her glasses with a pencil. Not one hair dared moved out of its appointed place.

"Please," Lane said.

"Take a seat." She let out a long, exasperated sigh.

Lane found a seat near the window and looked out at the trees and rooftops across the street.

"Read to me." A big little voice said. A bright yellow book dropped into his lap.

The child standing in front of him was between three and four years of age. Her black hair was cut short. It framed brown eyes and a round face. She wore blue Oshkosh coveralls and a red T-shirt. Slapping the book with her right hand, she climbed onto the seat beside him.

Lane looked across at a woman who smiled wearily. An infant slept in her arms.

He smiled, lifted the book and began to read. After the third book, the little girl announced, "I'm Dayna."

"I'm Lane."

"Read another story." Dayna scampered to a pile of books in the corner, picked three and brought them back.

"*Millicent and the Wind*," he said, as she put both hands on his wrist and leaned in to study the pictures. Lane ached for the children he would never have.

"Mr. Lane?" Lane lifted his head to see Mavis, Dr. Keeler's nurse. Shrinking violet had never been a phrase used to describe Mavis. She was taller than he was, broader in the shoulders and as tough as any person made out of marshmallow could be. "Hurry it up detective."

"Bye Dayna," Lane stood, looked down.

The child looked up with a frown. "Bye." She waved by closing and opening her fist.

"Say thank you," Dayna's mother said.

"But he didn't finish all my stories!" Dayna said.

Lane followed Mavis. He felt like a car being pulled along by the draft of a semi.

"He's not too busy just yet, so you're lucky." Mavis led him to the doctor's office and swept Lane inside with the folder in her hand. "Another case?"

"That's right." This was a familiar routine for Mavis and Lane. He'd first seen Keeler because he was a top-notch family doctor, and later on to ask medial questions related to his cases. All he had to do was phone ahead and Keeler would work him in. Amateur sleuths were everywhere and this one happened to offer invaluable medical insights. "Mavis, you're a life saver."

"Yah right, save your charm for Arthur." Her voice softened. "The doctor'll be here in a minute."

Lane sat in one of the chairs in front of the doctor's desk. He studied the photographs on top of the pine bookshelf behind the desk. An eight-by-ten was a family shot of the doctor, his daughter, son, and wife. All were taller than the doctor.

"Detective?" Keeler always used the title when it involved a case. He stood in the doorway dressed in a white smock and red golf shirt.

Lane was reminded of the face of a writer who loved ghosts and gore.

Keeler shook Lane's hand and said, "I've got maybe three minutes." He shut the door behind him before sitting down across from Lane. Keeler kept his hands on the arms of the chair while studying the detective.

Dr. Keeler always seems to enjoy this so much, Lane thought, then said, "I'm working on a case."

"We've done this at least fifty times before and you always start the same way." Keeler tapped his wristwatch with an index finger.

"How much damage can a blow to the throat cause?"

"Depends on where the blow lands, the power of it, and the size of the person or persons involved." Keeler leaned forward.

"Apparently, the attacker had a knife to the nose of an adolescent male. The attacker," Lane deliberately used the present tense even though he was almost certain that past would have been more accurate, "weighs about 140 kilos. His age is 53. The victim is close to the same height and weighs about 85 kilos. The victim says he," Lane curled the forefinger of his right hand over top of his index finger and jabbed both in Keeler's direction, "struck the attacker in the throat. Apparently, the attacker fell forward on top of the victim."

"The Swatsky case?" Keeler said.

"You understand this is entirely confidential?"

"Of course. Go on."

"The victim has studied karate and I suspect he's having flashbacks about the attack. There is also evidence suggesting the attack was sexually motivated. There are indications the attacker may have committed at least one prior assault similar to this one."

Keeler opened the collar of his golf shirt to expose his throat. He pressed his finger on the V at the base of his neck. "Feel that?"

Lane reached under his tie, eased his fingers between two buttons and felt a soft valley of flesh in between bones.

"If the blow landed there with sufficient force, then the attacker is a dead man. Fractured trachea. About ten years ago I was working at Emergency. A car accident happened right outside the door. A passenger fractured his trachea. We were there within thirty seconds. The guy never had a chance."

"A kid could do that?" Lane needed to be certain.

"If the blow lands in the right spot and with enough force, it's all over," Keeler said.

"And it's quick?"

"Very. Is the kid strong?"

"Yes."

"Then it's distinctly possible that the attacker is dead."

"Thank you," Lane reached across to shake hands. "And you understand . . . "

"Very confidential, as always. One of my male patients was sexually abused by an uncle. He's been in therapy for five years. The emotional damage can be irreparable."

"It's my job to find out what happened."

"What happens to the kid?" Keeler said.

"That's up to the courts to decide."

"You think so? This is the kind of case people can't get enough of." Keeler shook Lane's hand.

⚓

"v Channel news and weather update." The woman with the black hair, white blouse, and microphone stood on the bank of the Bow River. The white stone of the Louise Bridge was in the background. "It may be sunny in Calgary but it's raining in the mountains."

A closer shot of the bridge with water churning around the supports followed. Debris carried by the silty water was only a metre or two away from rubbing against the under-belly of the bridge.

Cut to the reporter. "Conditions on the Bow River are exceptionally dangerous. The fire department is warning boaters to stay off the river until conditions improve. So, you can't cool off on the river for the next few days. If that makes you hot under the collar what's next will really steam you. Here's Ralph Devine with a story about a major crime."

Cut to a head and shoulders shot of a man with black hair and salt-and-pepper beard. "The Swatsky disappearance may cost Red Deer taxpayers more than they thought. Investigators now believe the missing mayor may have gotten away with as much as 13 million dollars. More at six."

CHAPTER 22

Lester sat on The Racquet Club steps close to the front entrance. The sun shone on the bricks, which radiated heat and barbecued him like a bratwurst. He read yesterday's newspaper. It had been on the table at Tim Horton's when they went for breakfast. That was over four hours ago.

They chose The Racquet Club because it was in one of the wealthier districts. Marv had been sure it gave them a better chance of stealing a Mercedes. God, my brother is a pain in the ass, Les thought. "It's gotta be a Mercedes, or it'll all go wrong," Marvin had said. Les was beginning to think jail would be better than another day with his brother.

The newspaper front page had "Heat Wave" written across the top. He looked over the paper as a green minivan made a U-turn in front of him. The side door slid open. Four kids in bathing suits and sandals poured out. A woman's voice hollered, "I'll pick you up in two hours!" The last kid slammed the door.

In a couple of minutes those kids would be screaming and splashing in the pool. He could hear children in the water just on the other side of the entranceway.

Someone had to pull up, leave the car running and go inside. He'd done it lots of times. Just one person needed to do the same for him. Lester had only seen six Mercedes so far. Lots of minivans, though. Hate those minivans! Give me a Cadillac anytime. Big engine, leather seats, cruise, air conditioning, he thought.

A motorcycle climbed the parking lot hill and eased into a spot only a few metres from Les. The rider kicked out the stand, leaned the bike over and killed the engine. The guy was wearing a short-sleeved shirt, shorts, runners, and helmet. He pulled the helmet off and walked past Les. Cool as a cucumber.

Man, Les thought, that's the way to travel. A Honda Gold Wing with the highway stretching out ahead of him. A friend of his travelled down to the States every summer. Packed his pistol on his hip and rode his bike from coast to coast. It would be cool on a bike. Get a Gold Wing and ride down to the States. A man could still be a man down there and ride with a nine millimetre on his hip.

He heard the howl of an engine. It was the green minivan. The driver braked, leaned into a U-turn so tight the tires rubbed themselves bald. The van rocked back and forth when the driver dropped it into park before stopping. A woman hopped out with a plastic shopping bag with a towel trailing from the top. She ran into the club.

Les folded his newspaper and tucked it under his arm. Looking in the rear windows to make sure there was no one inside, he moved closer to the front of the vehicle. Empty. He opened the driver's door. Cool air enveloped him. Les smiled as he leaned to slide the seat back. He closed the door, shifted into drive, and eased his way down the hill. "After we get the money, I may just get me one of these."

~

The only kind of sandwich Nanny would eat was made of white bread and ham. And a cup of black coffee. "Make sure you don't put nothin' in my coffee but coffee," she'd said. It was early afternoon and the kitchen was cool. He'd kept the blinds and curtains closed like she'd told him. Ernie wondered why she hadn't made him feel guilty about going away with his father. She'd be alone during the day and she hated being alone. Last night she'd insisted he drive home. She was definitely getting weirder.

"Just keep busy, try to think about something else," Ernie said.

Scout lay under the kitchen table with her nose on her paws and her belly on the linoleum. Her eyes followed Ernie.

"Cooler, isn't it girl?"

Scout wagged her tail once in reply.

Ernie turned to butter the bread. Carefully, he spread yellow to the edges of the crust, just the way his grandmother liked it. "She's really acting strange. Well, she always acts strange." Talking to Scout was easy. She listened and he couldn't say the wrong thing. If he talked to her, maybe he wouldn't have time to think about other things. He peeled off two slices of honey ham and centred them on the bread. "When Nanny's this nice, it's really strange."

Ernie looked over his shoulder at the dog. She lifted one eyebrow.

"You're right. People are crazy. Dogs aren't."

Scout yawned.

"Humans think they're the smart ones. How come we're so screwed up if we're so smart?" He squirted a bead of mustard over the ham and slapped the sandwich together. Reaching into the opaque plastic pouch, he pulled out a slice of ham and jammed it into his mouth. It tasted like paste. He poured the coffee and wondered how something that smelled so good just a few days ago could taste like nothing today. Why does everything taste the same? He headed for his grandmother's bedroom. When his feet touched the family room carpet, he heard the rattle of toenails on a hard surface. "Oh no."

Scout had her front paws on the edge of the counter. Her tongue reached out and licked the ham out of the package. "Scout!" The ham slapped the floor. Scout picked it up and scampered into the front room. "What if I want to make another sandwich?"

Ernie turned and walked upstairs to Nanny's room. Fatigue scratched at the insides of his eyelids.

Nanny was exactly where she'd been since morning.

"Here's your lunch," Ernie said.

"Thanks," she said without looking at him.

Fear and lack of sleep forced the words out before he had time to think. "What do I do if he comes back?"

"Who?" Nanny said.

"Uncle Bob. What if he comes after me again?" Ernie slumped onto the edge of the bed.

"Oh, him." She reached for her cigarettes.

Ernie looked at the pile of butts and ash.

She stuck a fresh smoke in her mouth and spoke through partially closed lips. "He's not coming back. Don't worry about him."

"How do you know?"

"I know." Nanny blew smoke through her words, "He's not coming back."

"Then why am I having these nightmares? I can't sleep." He crossed his arms and rubbed goose bumps.

"Come here." She waved him closer. "Bob isn't coming back. He can't hurt you anymore."

"Sometimes, even when I'm awake, I see that knife in front of my eyes and I can smell him, hear his voice." He tasted ham and stomach acid at the back of his throat.

"I had those too."

Ernie waited. She never took her eyes off the road. A white pickup truck breezed by. "That guy lives down the street," she said.

"Who are you watching for?"

Nanny ignored the question and told him something he hadn't heard before. "Getting the news about my brother dying in Italy wasn't when the nightmares started."

Ernie opened his mouth to ask what this had to do with anything, hesitated, then decided to wait.

"It was later, when the boys came back after the war. I kept looking for him. Then one of the guys came to the house and told us how my brother died."

Ernie looked at the head and shoulders portrait of Nanny's uniformed brother.

"Had nightmares after that. You know he was burned alive?" A blue car approached and she lifted the binoculars. She set the binoculars in her lap. "The nightmares lasted at least a year. I swore no one would ever take family away from me again." She crushed the cigarette butt on the edge of the ashtray. "Then Bob took my Judy away."

Her anger was as familiar to him as her menopausal mustache.

"Couldn't do a damned thing about it. Judy wouldn't listen when I told her he was no good for her. Now his tough friends are back. They won't leave until they find Bob. No way they're gonna take anyone else away from me." She turned to look at him. "Don't worry about Bob or his tough friends. Take the dog and go into the basement. Have a sleep on the couch. It's cooler down there. Nightmares don't like the cold."

Ernesto knelt at the edge of his garden. "All done. No more weeds." Nasturtiums, gladiolas, tiger lilies, and wildflowers accented tomatoes, onions, and lettuce. The soles of his feet were black like his fingers.

His knees crackled when he leaned up against the garage to stand up. He looked at Nonna sitting at the table. "You want me to move you under the umbrella?" He bent to brush the soil off the knees of his jeans. "The sun does feel good this time of day." Ernesto shaded his eyes and looked up. The sun was nearly halfway along on its glide into sunset. "Must be close to five o'clock." He lifted his white ball cap. "Got fresh tomatoes, lettuce, onions, and some olives for a salad." He felt newly cut grass between his toes. Stepping lightly, he went up the stairs and disappeared into the doorway's shadow. "Just a quick stop in the bathroom to clean up."

Ernesto didn't hear the gate latch open.

❧

Nanny spotted Lester and Marvin sitting side by side in a green van.

The van turned right. The brake lights told her what she needed to know. "Ernesto's," she said while flipping open her cigarette package to check for the lighter. She dropped the pack into her purse and pulled out a white envelope to set on the bed. "I knew the sneaky bastards would be back." Glancing once at the portrait of her brother, she picked up her purse, shuffled across the carpet, and went downstairs. "Goddamn war killed my brother. Goddamned Bob. Goddamn his tough friends. Goddamn." She switched over to the portable oxygen tank. "Goddamn cigarettes! So damn short of breath." She wished she could go into the basement and touch Ernie's cheek one more time while he slept.

Nanny stepped outside and into the shadow of the house. Ever since she started to take those blood thinners, she couldn't stand the heat. "Damn!" The sun was a hand smacking her face. It was hard to breathe so she cursed to herself, Goddamn heat. Why couldn't those assholes park closer to the house? Took away my Judy. All I had was my family and you bastards took that away! Her rage pushed her till she stood beside the van and heaved the oxygen tank inside the open side door.

❖

Marv sat in the driver's set of the green van. He thought, Lester doesn't understand. This van was no good. It had to be a Mercedes. Without the right car, their luck would turn bad.

He looked over his shoulder at the open door. It was just the way Les wanted it for a quick getaway. They'd snatch the doll. All they had to do was kidnap the doll and find out what the old man knew about Bob. This way they didn't have to deal with Bob's crazy mother-in-law.

The van leaned to the right. "Les?" Marvin said and looked over his shoulder. Bob's mother-in-law, her hands on either side of the open door, pulled herself inside.

"What?" Marv reached to push her back out but the seat belt held him. He reached for the release. "What the hell?"

"What," she said. Each word was separated by a breath, "the . . . hell . . . did . . . you . . . think . . . I'd . . . do?"

They were face to face. Leona held her purse with both hands and slid her backside across to the middle of the back seat.

"Get out!" Marvin said.

"Told . . . you . . . two to . . . leave . . . me . . . and mine . . . alone." She shifted left till she sat behind him. Sweat soaked her T-shirt.

Marv felt a growing sense of doom. First the Mercedes and now this. The plan was going to hell.

"What the hell is she doin' here?" Les' face was running with sweat. He held the doll by the hair. "Get her out of here!"

Marv fought with the seat belt.

Leona pulled hers across her body and locked herself in. *Blatt!*

"What was that?" Marv said.

"You've never heard a fart before?" Les said as he sat the doll down on the floor.

"Sonamabitch!" Ernesto said.

Les shoved the doll inside. Her head caught Leona on the knee.

"Ouch!" Leona said as Lester slid the door shut.

"Go!" Lester clawed his way into the front seat.

Marv punched the accelerator. The engine screamed.

"Put it in gear, stupid!" Les slammed the door on his ankle. "Shit!" He dragged his foot inside.

Marv shifted into drive before completely releasing the accelerator, and the van lunged forward with squealing tires. He wrenched the steering wheel left. The passenger door's mirror snapped when it clipped the back of the red van.

"You all right?" Marv said.

"Shut up!" Les winced when he shifted his weight. "Just get us away from here so we can dump the old bitch!"

"What about him?" Marv jerked his thumb toward the back of the van.

Les leaned forward to look out the passenger mirror. It flopped like a hand with a broken wrist. He turned to look out the back window. The red van was gaining. "Lose him."

Leona lifted the glass jar of gasoline out of her purse and set it upright between her legs. She took quick gulps of bottled oxygen and leaned against the window.

"Take the main road!" Les said. They joined six lanes divided by concrete barriers.

Les adjusted the interior mirror so he could watch Ernesto. "You just worry about what's ahead and I'll worry about him."

"It's turning yellow!" Marv said.

Les glanced at the road ahead. "Good! Just go!"

Leona saw the light turn red before they entered the intersection. A silver car saw them just in time. Brakes screamed.

Les watched the red van. It had no choice but to brake. Blue smoke spilled out around the tires.

"That'll do it. Only two or three more sets of lights before we hit the river. Get in the right lane." Les adjusted the rear-view mirror so he could see Leona's eyes. "Why'd you let her in here?"

"She just climbed in," Marv said.

"Shit!" His ankle was throbbing and the pain made it harder to think, to plan ahead.

Blattt!

"Jeez Marv!" Les said.

"It wasn't me!"

"Yah, right."

They hit a green light and Les saw the sign for Memorial Drive. "That's our turn."

"You said two lights!"

"Just take the right lane." With the way his ankle was throbbing, Lester wouldn't be able to drive even if he had to.

"Look out!" Marv said.

⚜

Ernesto shivered.

"Never again!" He swerved into the right lane and passed a city bus.

"No bastard's gonna do this to you!"

⚜

"He's behind us!" Marv said.

"Watch out!" Les slapped his brother on the shoulder and pointed ahead. A backhoe, doing about half the speed limit, bounced on huge tires. The bucket at the back of the tractor was less than two car lengths ahead.

Marv swerved right and cut off a pickup truck.

A horn blared.

Les leaned into the turn. They flashed past the yellow tractor. "Watch the road like I told you!"

Marv accelerated to join the traffic on Memorial Drive.

Ernesto pulled up less than a car length behind them.

"Don't panic, Marv." Les pulled the Smith and Wesson out of its holster. "When you see an open stretch of road, let him pull up on my side."

Marv looked ahead. Trees lined the right side of the road. In between the road and the river, joggers and cyclists navigated the paved pathway. They were the fourth vehicle behind a group of cars. Ernesto trailed them. They passed through an intersection with the Louise Bridge on their right.

A car in the left lane slowed. They passed on the right.

"Get in the left lane," Les ordered and opened the window. "Let him get nice and close."

❧

Ernesto saw the green van pull into the left lane. The passenger window opened halfway. The broken mirror flapped against the door.

"Culo!" He swerved to drive alongside.

❧

"He's almost beside us!" Marv said.

They ran over a manhole cover.

Les fired one round. A star appeared in the center of Ernesto's windshield. "Shit! I missed."

"He's pulled in behind us," Marv said.

"Watch the road!" Les looked ahead. Now I have to figure out something else, he thought. The road curved right. Centre Street Bridge arched its sandstone back over the water. Suspended beneath, a steel bridge hung above the swollen river. "Get in the right lane."

"What you gonna do?" Marv said.

"The old guy wants his doll. We'll give him his doll. We still have the old bitch. I'll bet she knows where Bob is if anyone does."

"You said the old man would be a pushover," Marv said.

"You won't believe me when I tell you where Bob is," Leona said.

"Just turn right under the bridge and do what I tell you. We'll get rid of the old man and then we'll find out what this old bitch knows."

Marv braked for a red light. A white Mazda sat between them and a right turn.

Les held the rearview mirror in his hand as Ernesto opened his door.

Leona fumbled with the lid of the jar.

The light turned green.

Marv lurched forward.

Leona screwed the lid back down tight.

They turned right. The bridge deck was narrow. Tires hummed on the irregular, perforated metal surface. "I don't like this," Marv said.

A taxi passed going the other way. No other vehicles approached. "Stop in the middle of the road," Les said.

"Why?"

"I won't be able to get out and throw the doll over if you don't stop in the middle."

"Why?" Marv said.

"Do it!"

Marv hit the brakes and swung the wheel to the left. The van straddled the centre line.

Les leaned into the damaged passenger door. Pain clawed at him when he put weight on his right foot. "Shit!" He heaved the van's side door open, grabbed the doll by the back of its dress, twisted its arm at the elbow and limped to the edge. He heaved her over the side.

"NO!" Ernesto was crossing to the other side of the bridge. He looked at the green van once.

Leona shuddered as she heard the cry of a man ripped open by grief.

The old man heaved himself up to the railing and jumped into the river.

Les pulled himself into the van. He lifted his right leg inside. The door would only close part way. He heaved to slam it shut. "Get us out of here!"

"You bastards." Leona shook her head.

"He's just a dirty old man. Turn left and get us back onto Memorial," Les said.

"You ruined my family, and now you've killed Ernesto," Nanny said.

⌘

Ernesto bobbed to the surface. The shock of hitting the water stunned him.

The current carried him while he searched the surface. His foot smashed painfully against rock. He saw her hair first. Just under the surface. Ernesto swam to her and grabbed. Her face surfaced. By this time his feet were pointing downstream. He held her hair in his teeth and used his arms to keep them floating. They passed under a bridge. A pair of faces stared down at him and were gone.

Ernesto locked her arms around his neck. "Helen?" No answer. "Talk to me."

The water seemed warmer now. He thought about their holiday in Italy and cooling off in the Mediterranean. It hadn't been so long ago. "Remember our big trip? Remember how warm the water was? I can see that dress you wore."

"Hold on to me," she said.

He remembered the sea. Helen's face inches from his. Looking up at the sky, he thought about how perfect their honeymoon had been.

A steel cable caught him on the right side of the head. The shock of the blow knocked him out. They rolled beneath the surface then over the concrete weir. In a moment they were caught in a churning prison of white water. It turned them over and over till all the oxygen escaped Ernesto's lungs.

⁂

"Take the Deerfoot north. That way we'll get there faster." Les pointed, directing Marvin.

"It was you two who threw the rock through our store window." Leona lit a cigarette.

"Gimme a cigarette," Les said and reached back with an open hand.

"Answer first." She took a drag.

"What the hell are you asking?" Les said.

"Our store. You two helped ruin our business when my Judy ran away."

"That was a long time ago," Les said.

Leona waited and watched him through a filter of exhaled smoke.

"The rock was Bob's idea. Said it would scare you." Les wiggled his fingers and she dropped a cigarette into his palm.

"How about the slashed tires?" she said.

Marv looked at Les who searched for the cigarette lighter. "I need a light."

"Answer the question and I'll light it for you." She glanced left to see the jar in the cup holder. The gasoline quivered. Cars, pickup trucks, and semis passed them on either side as they headed north on the freeway.

"Judy was right, you are a controlling old bitch." Les put the cigarette between his lips.

Leona took a breath to keep her mind clear for what she had to do. This is what I should have done when they took my Judy away, she thought.

"Yah, we did it. Bob paid us twenty bucks for that one." He reached back for the light.

Leona lit another cigarette with the tip of hers and handed it to him. "What about the letter to Beth?"

Les looked at his brother. He took a long drag on the cigarette, blew smoke out his nostrils and said, "I'm real good at letters."

Leona nodded.

"Judy helped me write it."

"Judy?" Leona said.

"Sure. Then she tried to get Beth to run away with her to teach you a lesson."

Leona thought, Beth never told me. Never told me while she gained all that weight. No wonder! No goddamned wonder she hates Judy. She looked out the left window. A silver blue semi was pulling up alongside. It struggled as they climbed a gentle incline. "Where we goin' now?"

"Back to your place. You'll tell us whatever we want to know. All I have to do is put my gun up against the side of the boy's head."

You're not gonna get anywhere near Ernie, she thought. "And if I call the police after you leave?"

Les said, "We'll come back. Marv, we gotta get off this road pretty soon. Get in the right lane."

"Can't," Marv said.

On the right, a white semi rolled up beside them.

"Slow down, then," Les said.

Marv pointed back with his thumb. The headlights and grill of a black one tonne pickup filled the rear window.

"Speed up," Les pointed.

Leona threw her cigarette on the floor. She pulled the oxygen tube over her head and dropped it. The lid of the jar opened easily. Nanny leaned forward and poured half the gas down the back of Marv's golf shirt.

"What?" He leaned forward. "What the hell are you doin'?"

Les turned.

She flicked the remainder into his face.

"My eyes! Gas! For Christ's sake, she's got gas!"

She reached into her purse. The oxygen tubes lay next to it. She put a smoke in her mouth and lifted the lighter.

"My eyes!" Les said.

Leona lifted the lighter and flicked the wheel. She leaned to touch it against Marv's shoulder. Flame traveled across the back of his neck. Gasoline ignited on her hand. She saw the flames spread to Les's face. Both men screamed.

Marv swerved into the left lane.

The van buried its nose under the trailer.

CHAPTER 23

"Ernie!" Beth shook his shoulder.

The dog growled.

"Don't you growl at me, Scout! Ernie wake up. Where's Nanny?"

Ernie's mind was taking the long way back to consciousness. He opened his eyes and saw his mother. She was wiping her face with the back of her hand. The front of her white blouse was spotted where tears had fallen and turned the fabric translucent. Scout's lip was curled back to reveal teeth. "Scout, stop that," he said. The dog wagged her tail, ducked her head and moved closer to lick his face. Ernie sat up, wiping the back of his hand across his lips. "What's wrong, Mom?"

"She's gone and she left this on her bed!" Beth waved a white envelope.

"What's that?" Ernie had never seen his mother like this, even during the divorce. He rubbed Scout under the chin, then the dog went to Beth and licked her free hand.

"A note. And money. Lots of money."

"She told me to come down here and sleep. Said nightmares don't like the cold. She was acting weird all morning. Wouldn't leave her room. Watched all the cars coming and going." Ernie stood.

"She's never done this before." Beth's chin fell to her chest and her son wrapped an arm around her shoulders.

They went up the stairs. Ernie left her in the kitchen where the electric kettle began to boil. He took the stairs two at a time to the second floor. In his grandmother's room, the plate and coffee cup sat empty on the end table with the mountain of cigarette butts and the binoculars. He checked each upstairs room after that. Coming downstairs, he noticed the oxygen machine continued to hum in the hallway. Air bubbled through the clear plastic container of water at the side of the machine.

"I'll phone Nonno to see if he knows anything." Ernie picked up the phone and dialed.

"I'll check the backyard." Beth moved to the deck door.

"Ten, he always picks up the phone before ten rings even when he's in the back yard." Ernie waited for twelve rings before hanging up.

The screen door opened and Beth stepped back in.

"She there?" Ernie said.

Beth shook her head.

"No other note?" He looked for one on the kitchen table.

"Nope, I checked."

"She take the car?"

"I drove it to work today." Beth turned toward the kettle. The water boiled.

"I'll go to Nonno's and check there. You want to stay here?"

She poured steaming water into the tea pot, "Don't take too long."

Lane leaned over and rubbed Riley behind the ears before the retriever would allow him to enter the back yard. "How's the nose?" He looked closer to see how it was doing. "You sure heal fast." Riley wagged his tail.

After the gate was closed, Riley pranced ahead, then returned to hurry Lane along.

"I know, we've got a visitor. I saw the car parked out front," Lane said.

When they rounded the side of the house, he saw Arthur wearing a purple satin shirt and baggy black satin pants. Where did he get those? Lane thought, before he noticed Arthur wasn't wearing shoes.

Arthur always wore shoes. And he sat back in his chair, one leg hanging over the other and his left hand resting on the top knee. His right hand was suspended horizontally and bent ninety degrees at the wrist.

Harper was still in his uniform; including a tie. Lane was glad to see he wasn't wearing a Glock. The officer sat still, back straight as a baton, feet firmly on the ground and both hands on the arms of the chair. It appeared he had some difficulty fitting his football player body into the lawn chair. He looked at Lane and smiled with more than a little bit of apprehension.

Lane looked beyond them to the fence where, in between the vertical boards, he could see a silhouette. He joined the visible dots of yellow cotton fabric and flesh into a mental image of Mrs. Smallway. Somehow, he couldn't yet bring himself to accept the fact that she was a swinger.

"Oh, he's home." Arthur stood and minced his way to Lane. Riley sniffed the air near Arthur as if trying to identify this human he knew intimately but had never seen like this before. Arthur grabbed Lane's shoulders and landed kisses on either cheek.

"What the hell is going on?" Lane whispered.

"Just having a bit of fun," Arthur whispered back. "Play along."

Lane smiled.

"I'll get supper." Arthur said to Harper. "You behave yourself."

Lane took off his jacket and draped it over the back of his chair. He poured himself a tumbler full of iced tea, then filled up Harper's glass. "Hello Mrs. Smallway!" Lane said.

The volume caused the birds in the tree to stop chirping.

"Lovely evening isn't it Mrs. Smallway?" Lane was sure someone in the yard six houses down would soon answer if Mrs. Smallway didn't.

"Oh, is that you Mr. Lane?" This was followed by the snip of pruning shears on a twig. "Just doing a little work in the yard."

Lane grinned at Harper. Lane said, "Mrs. Smallway doesn't 'do' gardening. She hires people to do that sort of work." Then he increased the volume, "Beautiful evening for it!"

"Best be getting inside and out of the sun! Nice talking to you!" Mrs. Smallway said.

Lane waited till he heard Mrs. Smallway's screen door close. He sat, looked at Harper, mouthed the word, "Wait," and pointed to a window with a view of Lane's backyard. There was the sound of running water, then silence.

"I think she sits on the toilet and eavesdrops for hours. One of these days we'll have to call the paramedics when her legs go to sleep."

"Who spends all of the time on this garden?" Harper looked around him.

"We both do."

"I took up gardening after the shooting and I must say I'm hooked. Surprised?"

"No," Lane said.

Harper lowered his voice, "I found out a few things this afternoon."

"We have to wait for Arthur."

Arthur backed out the door carrying a tray, salad bowl, black pepper mill, and three plates. As he set tray and contents onto the table, Lane said, "He's got some fresh information to share."

Harper looked sideways at Lane.

Lane nodded at Harper, "The chief wants you to know how I solve crimes. Since I haven't had a department partner, Arthur has become mine."

Arthur's face became a study in concentration as he dished out salad on each plate. He sat, stabbed at his salad, lifted tomato, black olive, and feta cheese to his mouth and waited for Harper to begin.

"I checked to find out who was buried at Queen's Park Cemetery the day Swatsky disappeared. Two burials in the morning and three in the afternoon. Seems the morning burials all happened before lunch and none of the afternoon burials began before 1:30 PM. A service in the afternoon caught my eye." He opened a notepad and put it faceup on the table. He pointed at a name.

"You've got to be kidding." Arthur dropped the affected accent and looked across the table at Lane.

Harper glanced at Arthur as if something had just occurred to him.

Lane smiled when he realized Harper was beginning to see through Arthur's foppish facade.

"I also found out that the RCMP are looking for Lester and Marvin Klein. Two brothers who have been long time business associates of Swatsky. Apparently, they have been traced to this city. They're connected to this 13 million dollar land scam."

Arthur cut in, "Where were the Klein brothers sighted?"

"Motel Village near McMahon Stadium." Harper took a sip of iced tea before lifting his fork.

"What's eating at you?" Arthur said to Lane.

"I went to see Keeler."

"Who's Keeler?" Harper said with his mouth full.

"A doctor I confer with from time to time," Lane said.

Harper swallowed. "Forensic?"

"Family medicine."

Harper smiled.

"What?" Lane said.

Harper looked at Arthur and back to Lane.

"Don't think, just answer the question." Arthur smiled in an attempt to soften the bluntness of his words.

"I wasn't sure what to expect when I came here. I mean you have no reason to invite me into your house after what I said to you. In fact, I was surprised you didn't put up a fight when I requested to be your partner. So, I kept telling myself not to come here with preconceptions. I'm smiling because of your performance, Arthur."

Arthur bowed.

"Making a partner a partner is a novel idea," Harper continued to smile as he spoke, "and using a family doctor is another . . . " he searched for the right word.

"Novel approach?" Arthur completed the sentence for him. "Why the change?"

"What change?" Harper said.

"Since the night you were shot and the horrible things you said to Lane," Arthur said.

Lane shifted in his chair, uncomfortable with the question yet anxious for the answer.

"My nephew, Chris, took an overdose of drugs," Harper looked at his salad.

Arthur set his fork silently on his plate.

Lane studied Harper's face.

"At the time, Chris was sixteen. He's my older sister's son. I watched him grow up. My brother-in-law kicked Chris out when he came out."

"How long ago?" Arthur said.

"About three months after Lane found me on that front step. My nephew came to live with us. That's when my education began. Chris still lives with us, by the way."

Lane reached into his pocket and pulled out a pager. He lifted it to eye level. "I'd better take this."

Arthur lifted his eyebrows.

"It's Rapozo." Lane pushed his chair back. "I really have to take this."

Arthur turned to Harper, "I'll be deeply offended if you don't at least try to finish your salad."

Harper smiled and hefted his fork.

Lane stepped inside the back door and into the kitchen. He sat at the table, picked the phone off the wall and slid pen and paper closer. He dialed. It rang once, "Ms. Rapozo, it's Detective Lane."

"You said not to hesitate to call. I can't find my mother and Ernesto, my father-in-law, isn't at home. A couple of Bob's buddies were by a few days ago. They tried to intimidate my mother and then sent a disgusting letter. I'm afraid," Beth said.

Lane heard the fear in her voice and kept his tone even. "My impression is that she's quite sharp mentally. Is that an accurate assessment?"

"Sometimes too sharp," Beth said.

"You mentioned two of Bob's buddies."

"Yes, they're too old friends of Bob's. Named Lester and Marvin."

"Klein?" Lane said.

"How'd you know?" Beth said.

"A . . ." He felt the bits of evidence coming together. He said, "Anything else unusual happen?"

"Mom's been sitting up in her room the last couple of days, watching out the window."

Lane waited.

"Watching for the Three Stooges."

"Three Stooges?" Lane said.

"Sorry. That's what I call Bob, Les, and Marv."

"Why not contact me after they came to the house and sent the letter?"

"Mom said it wouldn't do any good. She said it didn't help twenty-five years ago and the police wouldn't be able to help this time."

"What happened twenty-five years ago?" Lane said.

"My sister ran away. Around that time our house, the truck, our business, were all vandalized. Rumours were spread around town. People stopped coming to the store. Mom and Dad had to sell out. Ever live in a small town?"

"Nope."

"The rumours start and it's hard to stop them. Later on, we found out that Bob got Lester and Marvin to do most of the dirty work but there was no way to prove it."

Lane waited for her to continue.

"Mom said she'd take care of it herself. I didn't really listen. I mean, in her condition, what could she do?"

"Anything else?"

"She left an envelope up in her room. Addressed to me," Beth said.

"What did it say, exactly?"

There was the sound of rustling paper and then, "To

Beth. Love Mom. Then a phone number. And $10,000 in cash."

"That much?"

"Mom didn't spend much."

"Whose phone number?" Lane said.

"When I dialed, it turned out to be Ridley's Funeral Home. She prepaid her funeral expenses."

Lane saw the pieces of this case like glass on the floor. After staring long enough, sometimes it was possible to see what everything looked like in the moments just before a shattering event.

"What do I do?" Beth said.

"Stay at home. Stay by the phone. Is Ernie there with you?"

"Yes," she said.

"Both of you stay home. Keep the dog inside with you. I'm going to make some calls. I'll get back to you before the evening is over."

"Thank you."

Lane thought, I wonder how much she knows about Bob? I mean, would she call me if she knew what happened to him?

Beth said, "One other thing. It bothered me at the time but living with my mother, I kind of got used to her erratic behaviour. She was looking for lighter fluid. Got me out of bed early. This morning, I think. I can't remember. Anyway, it bothers me now because Ernie told me what she said to Les and Marv."

"Yes?"

"She said she'd burn them if they came back to bother us again."

"I'll call you back this evening," Lane said.

"Thanks."

Lane hung up the phone and thought about their next move. He looked out the kitchen window and saw Harper and Arthur talking. The phone rang.

⚜

Arthur sat in the back seat of their Jeep. Lane drove and Harper squeezed into the passenger seat. Harper gathered information from his radio. They followed 9th Avenue east into Inglewood. The neighbourhood had decided to be trendy. Coffee shops, restaurants, and antique stores lined the avenue.

Arthur said, "I hope you're wrong. It could be someone else."

Harper said, "Ernesto's van was found abandoned on the Centre Street Bridge. The keys were in it. Witnesses say a woman was thrown over the side of the bridge by a man who pulled her out of a green van. Apparently, the driver of Ernesto's van was seen to jump into the river. Now there is a report of two bodies caught in the weir. Unfortunately, the facts are leading to one conclusion. Just to complicate matters, there are fatalities on Deerfoot Trail."

"There's a unit in front of Beth Rapozo's home?" Lane said.

"Yes, that's just been confirmed." Harper turned around and said to Arthur, "You're sure quiet."

"Lane's putting it all together. Just watch," Arthur said.

They turned down a residential street where prewar houses sat on narrow lots near the railway yards.

Blue, white, and red lights flashed. A cruiser blocked a white metal barricade. The officer turned away a cyclist and then an inline skater. The cyclist stopped, reached into his backpack and pulled out a cell phone. Lane lowered his window and held out his badge. The officer spotted Harper and waved them through. They drove down the bicycle path. Through the trees on the left, it was possible to see a cable and red buoys stretched across the river to prevent people in rafts or canoes from going over the weir. They reached a clearing. Lane pulled the Jeep off the paved path and onto the grass.

On the other side of the Bow River, they spotted a fire truck. Its inflatable boat was missing.

Lane stepped out. He looked around at the trees rising up ten and twenty metres above them. His gaze dropped back to the weir where water curved in a continuous muddy arc over the concrete barrier and fell two metres into a boiling froth. A danger sign showed a human form trapped in the cycling water at the base of the weir. "Hello." An officer stepped out of a white SUV. He was at least as tall as Lane, broad shouldered, and Asian.

Lane reached for his ID.

"Hello, Terry," Harper said and reached out to shake hands. "This is Detective Lane."

Lane shook hands, feeling oddly out of tune and wondering if Harper knew how rarely Lane had experienced this act of fellowship.

"What's the situation?" Harper said.

"They just pulled the bodies out of the water. They're around at the back of the ambulance," Terry said.

"Thanks," Harper said. He and Lane walked down to the edge of the river where a Zodiac was beached.

The male body lay on its back. Another, in a dress, lay face down on the male's chest. The female's arms were locked around the man's neck. Her hair covered his face. Two firefighters in wet suits stood next to the bodies. One said, "Never would have believed it if I hadn't seen it."

A redheaded paramedic bent to brush hair away from the man's face.

Lane recognized Ernesto.

The redhead said, "Never seen one of these love dolls before. You guys must have more experience with silicone and rubber than I do."

One of the firefighters said, "Bet you've got more experience with battery powered appliances."

Lane said, "Before you go too far, the family would likely appreciate it if you left the two of them together."

"You can identify him?" another firefighter said.

Lane stepped closer. The redhead backed away. Ernesto's brown eyes were empty. On the side of his face there was an angry mark stretching from forehead, across the cheekbone and onto the side of the chin. They always look so different in death, Lane thought. "Ernesto Rapozo. It was his van abandoned on the Centre Street Bridge."

"The love doll is his?" the redhead said.

"She is," Lane said.

The redhead allowed herself a satisfied smile and smirked in the general direction of the firefighters.

"We'll notify the family," Lane said.

"Guess all the perverts in town know one another," the male paramedic said.

Lane faced the sharp-featured male leaning against the ambulance. Lane could not remember ever having met the paramedic before.

Harper's reaction caught them all by surprise. "You aware of the City's policy on harassment?"

The paramedic's white skin paled and he stepped away from the ambulance.

"If I write you up right now, at the very least you'll lose

some pay." Harper turned but kept his eyes away from Lane. He marched past the bodies up toward the SUV and Terry.

Lane followed, wondering how he would tell Beth. It was one thing he rarely had to do. Most often he arrived after the bad news had been broken to loved ones.

"Terry?" Harper said, "Get the names of those paramedics for me will you?"

"Sure." Terry looked at Lane. "What happened?"

"A bit of bigotry." Lane said, thinking, I may get to like having a partner. "Do you want the name of the deceased?"

Terry opened his breast pocket, pulling out a notebook and pen.

"Rapozo, Ernesto." Lane spelled it. "We'll notify the family. Please, make sure that's made clear."

Terry nodded. Lane walked back to his Jeep.

Harper fumed in the passenger seat. Lane got in and closed the door.

"What happened?" Arthur said.

Lane said, "It's Ernesto's body."

"And?" Arthur said.

"Helen. That's what he called her. I don't expect many people will understand it, but she was real to him. He used to talk to her. I could swear she talked to him once or twice," Lane said.

Harper stared straight ahead.

Lane turned the key. "I've learned how to shut out bigots."

"That paramedic asshole was way out of line. He reminded me of my brother-in-law," Harper said.

Lane said, "Did you notice that Deerfoot Trail is still backed up?"

"According to the radio it's backed up even further south," Arthur said.

"Was there a fire?" Lane said.

"Want me to check?" Harper said.

"Please." Lane looked over his right shoulder as he backed up. He stopped and shifted into first.

Lane said, "Leona said she would burn them if they came back."

⁂

Harper said, "Deerfoot is backed up for four or five kilometres, we'll have to detour around."

They backtracked to the zoo then headed along Edmonton Trail. Harper talked into his radio then turned to talk with Lane and Arthur, "This is what I've got so far. Three confirmed fatalities but the bodies are badly burned. All fatalities were passengers in a van. The van was reported stolen early this afternoon. An investigation team is on the scene now."

Lane turned east onto 32nd Avenue, then left onto the northbound Deerfoot ramp. He eased around the traffic jam by driving over the curb and onto the grass. "Was one of the victims female?"

"Not sure," Harper said.

They looked ahead. Traffic was down to a single lane on the freeway. An officer directed traffic and glared angrily at them as they bumped along the grass and stopped. Three tow truck drivers leaned against the fender of one truck.

"I'll wait here," Arthur said.

Lane and Harper stepped out of the Jeep. A red-faced officer stormed around the front of a semi, "Move that . . ." He spotted Harper. "Thought you were reporters."

"What have you got so far?" Harper said.

"Besides a hell of a mess?" the officer said.

Lane smelled burnt flesh and hair. He thought, They should have listened to Leona.

"Check with her." The officer pointed at a white police van parked in front of the accident scene.

Lane looked at the wrecked van. It was crumpled up to the windshield. Scorched metal framed a melted mass of plastic and upholstery. Behind the wreck, a pickup leaned forward on a pair of flat front tires. Its bumper, grill, and hood were crumpled. Two semi-trailers had blackened sides. Paint had boiled in places. An oxygen bottle was wedged under the dual wheels of one of the trailers. Two officers circled the wreckage. One focused a camera. There was an intense flash of white light.

"Lane?" Harper waved him closer.

Lane moved to the police van.

Harper said, "This is Sergeant Stephens."

Lane looked at a woman who was at least thirty. She had her auburn hair braided at the back.

"Found this under one of the trailers." Stephens pointed at a black leather purse. "It was thrown clear." She opened the bag, carefully picked out a wallet, and set it down on a paper bag. "We've got three deceased. By the size of the two in the front, I'm assuming they were male. This probably belonged to the person found in the back seat. The body was smaller than the others." She slipped the driver's license out of a plastic sleeve. "Leona Rankin."

"We think the other two are Marvin and Lester Klein," Lane said.

Stephens looked at her rubber gloves.

"I'll write it down for you," Harper said. He pulled out a notebook.

"Thanks," Stephens said.

"Explaining this to the daughter won't be easy," Lane said.

"You are going to do that?" Harper said.

"We are," Lane said.

"Don't envy that duty." Stephens's face was a mask.

Harper reached to put the names in her breast pocket, turned red and dropped his hands.

Stephens smiled, "Just put it on the clipboard on the front seat if you don't mind. Oh, one thing that's unusual, it looks like an accelerant was used to start the fire."

"Anything else?" Lane said.

"By the look of the skid marks, the van hit that one first." She pointed at the blue semi. "Then it rolled onto its side and was hit by the pickup. The gas tank ruptured and that was that."

Lane looked at a sky turning orange. He turned to Harper, "We need to talk to Beth. I have to see her face when we give her the news. Then I'll know if she had anything to do with what happened to Swatsky."

"We also found this at the scene." Stephens pointed at a plastic bag with a pistol inside. "Smith and Wesson nine millimetre Sigma."

"Probably belonged to one of the Klein boys," Lane said. "You may want to do a ballistics check. And, just so you know, this will probably turn out to be a very big news event."

"Tell me about it. The reporters left in a big hurry. They were all excited about how some poor bastard drowned in the arms of his sex doll."

CHAPTER 24

"What's so funny?" Ernie said. He was wearing a new black shirt and pants bought especially for the funeral.

Beth brushed the lapel of her red jacket. "I was thinking about Mom. We went for a drive out in the bush just after Judy ran away. Used to go quite often in the spring when the leaves came out and in the fall when they turned. It started to rain. The road was pretty rough. We got stuck. Mom put Dad's big rubber boots on and got out to push. I can still see her face as she pushed against the hood. Dad worked the gas and clutch and we started to move back. Mom's eyes got real wide. Her hands slid off the hood and she disappeared. We kept backing up and there she was lying face down in the mud. I looked at my Dad, he looked at me. Mom rolled on her back and started to laugh. When I think of her in the mud and hear her laughing, it always makes me smile." Beth looked around the funeral home's reception room where elderly people talked and drank coffee.

"Look at her," Ernie said. His cousin, Lisa, stood next to the coffee urn. She wore black eyeshadow, a black blouse, black jacket, black skirt, black stockings, and black leather shoes. As people came up to refill their cups, Lisa smiled, held out a business card and said, "LEONA WAS MY GRANDMOTHER. MY BUSINESS IS LIFE, DEATH, AND TAXES." She handed a card to a woman. The woman muttered something in Italian.

"SORRY, I DIDN'T HEAR THAT," Lisa said.

"Donna de la notte!" The woman said and turned without taking the card.

"AUNTY, WHAT DID SHE SAY?"

"She called you a lady of the evening," Beth said.

Lisa considered this for a moment then smiled when she spotted the arrival of two men in suits.

"Can pick your friends but can't pick your relatives," Arthur said.

Beth said, "Who are you?"

"Arthur." He extended his hand and pulled her close. He was impeccably dressed in a single-breasted grey suit, rainbow tie, and blue shirt. He put his arms around her and hugged. Beth closed her eyes at this unexpected kindness.

"Arthur always says what's on his mind. We came to pay our respects," Lane said.

Arthur released her and turned, "You must be Ernie." They shook hands.

Beth opened her hand in an invitation for them to sit. "Thank you for coming. I didn't expect this." She wiped her eyes.

"My Dad had to leave right after the funeral. He had a business meeting," Ernie said.

Lane studied Ernie. Dark half circles lay on the boy's cheeks. He must have lost between five and ten kilos, Lane thought.

"How about something to eat?" Arthur said to Ernie.

"Not hungry." Ernie crossed his arms over his chest.

"Well, then come and help me find something good." Arthur took hold of Ernie's elbow.

"All right." Ernie stood.

"Lead the way," Arthur said.

"If anyone can get him to eat, Arthur can," Lane said.

"He's still having those nightmares. Woke up screaming at three this morning. He thinks Bob is coming back."

"That's not likely." Lane studied her.

"When you came to tell us what happened to my Mother and Ernesto, you watched me the way you're watching me now."

"You're very perceptive," Lane said.

"You wanted to see how I'd react?"

"That's right. I had to know."

"What?" Beth said.

"If you knew what happened to Bob."

"Well, what did happen to Bob?"

"Ummm . . ."

"Come on, out with it."

Lane glanced at Lisa handing out another of her business cards, oblivious to their conversation, "For one thing, I don't know for sure. For another, you've experienced a series of tragedies."

"I was convinced my mother was hiding something from me. So was Ernesto." Beth leaned closer to Lane, "What the hell are you holding back? There's no way I'm gonna lose my son too!"

"I don't know the truth. I only suspect it." Underestimating this family is a habit I have to kick, Lane thought.

"Then, what do you suspect?" Beth said.

"Will you answer a question?"

"If you'll give me some answers," Beth said.

"What's it been like dealing with the media?"

"This morning I got a call from a talk show. They wanted us to fly to Chicago to discuss Ernesto's relationship with the doll."

"What did you say?"

"Do you know how to swear in Italian?" Beth said.

"No."

"I swore at them in Italian."

"What about the newspapers?" Lane said.

"A couple of tabloids phoned to set up an interview and take some pictures."

"Let me guess, you swore at them in Italian?"

"It felt good to swear at someone. Miguel came home and wouldn't lift a finger to help with the arrangements. Now, he's using work as an excuse not to deal with all of this. I can't swear at him. Ernie doesn't need that. And I've had to put up with her for the last three days." She glanced in Lisa's direction. "She keeps hinting about an inheritance from her grandmother and how much she misses Nanny. So, when the tabloids call, I let them have it."

"If my suspicions are correct, then that's just a taste of what you can expect from the media."

"I can take the tabloids. I can take the talk shows. But I can't take losing my son. I'll fight to the death to take care of my kid," Beth said.

"I suspect there's been enough of that already."

"When do I get my answer?"

"I'll set it up."

Arthur and Lane argued in the Jeep on the way home from the funeral.

Lane said, "It's the only way. If I'm there when he talks to Beth and Ernie, then I have to do my job. If you're there, it's a different situation."

"And what if I refuse?" Arthur said.

"Can you see another way?"

"You're forgetting something."

"What's that?" Lane said.

"Harper."

"He doesn't have to know."

"Yes he does, he's your partner."

"You don't understand," Lane said.

"No, you don't understand. You've got a partner. Harper works with you. You can't shut him out like you've shut out most everyone else. It's time to trust someone besides me. You think you can do this on your own. You can't. Listen to what I'm saying to you. Harper's a different person now. Trust him." Arthur crossed his arms to say there was no point in discussing this further.

CHAPTER 25

Ernie blinked and held on, keeping his eyes closed for over a minute. Opening his right eye first, he saw dust dancing in the sunlight. He turned his face to the pillow and wiped the sweat from his forehead. He heard snoring rise from a whisper to a roar before falling to a wheeze.

"Lisa," he said. She'd moved in before the funeral, camped out in Nanny's room, and had shown no inclination to leave.

He couldn't escape the nightmare of his uncle and now there was Lisa, the walking nightmare. She filled up the house with her demands. "WHERE'S THE MILK? WHERE'S THE CEREAL? HAVEN'T YOU GOT ANY CORN FLAKES? ERNIE, GET ME A POP. IT'S SO HOT IN HERE. HOW COME YOU DON'T HAVE AIR CONDITIONING? WHAT'S FOR SUPPER? AUNTY BETH WHERE ARE THE SANITARY NAPKINS? WHAT DO YOU MEAN YOU'RE OUT? WHAT AM I SUPPOSED TO DO? MY MOTHER ALWAYS BOUGHT THE NAPKINS!" Ernie took to raiding Lisa's stash of candies. She'd put them under some of Nanny's clothes in a drawer and whenever the opportunity arose, he'd grab a handful and stuff them in his pocket. Lisa had begun to stand very close, sniffing his breath and saying, "ANYTHING TO CONFESS?"

Nightmares of Uncle Bob came every night. Sweat and the smell of onions stayed with him. Lisa had to have onions with every meal. She fried them, boiled them, or ate them raw. Even over the dusty, lingering scent of his grandmother's cigarettes, there was the ripe, thick, sharp stink of onions.

He pulled on sweats and a T-shirt. Ernie remembered the salads Nonno used to make: tomatoes, yellow peppers, cucumbers, lettuce, with vinegar and olive oil. Then he remembered onions. Nausea ground him down.

Scout lifted her head and stretched her front paws.

Ernie rubbed her under the chin. She followed him downstairs. He looked for the oxygen line before remembering it was one of the first things his mother had thrown out. Next, she tossed the cigarettes.

Wheeze!

He couldn't smell his grandmother anymore. Just onions. He closed his eyes and hoped when he opened them again, he wouldn't feel that itchy, annoying, rough, scratching against his eyeballs. For a day or two, crying had eased the irritation.

He opened the sliding glass door and let Scout out. He reached for the remote on the coffee table, pressed power, then sat on Nanny's love seat.

The news was on. "Love dolls and the men who buy them." The reporter didn't smile. Her eyes stared down the camera. Her black hair was parted down the middle and curled behind her ears. A shot of an ambulance pulling away with the Bow River weir in the background. Back to the reporter. "The recent drowning of a Calgary man has raised many questions about love dolls and men who spend up to $7,000 to buy them." Next a clip of a life-sized doll in a teddy sitting in a wooden crate. The reporter said, "More on v Channel at six."

Ernie pressed the power button. The picture faded. "Can't even watch TV anymore."

Scout scratched at the door.

Ernie stuffed the remote down between the cushions. "Let Lisa go crazy trying to find it."

He remembered the look on his mother's face when Lisa cried, "MY PARENTS SOLD THE HOUSE. NEW PEOPLE MOVED IN. WHERE AM I GONNA GO?"

Ernie let Scout in. She put her paws on his knee. He rubbed her under the chin. "How about a walk?" She ran for the back door, then ran back to see if he really meant it. Then she waited, tail sweeping the linoleum as he attached the leash to her collar and opened the deadbolt.

"TELEPHONE!" Lisa said.

Beth rolled over and looked at the ceiling.

"TELEPHONE!"

Beth blinked and had her feet on the floor before she had time to think.

"TELEPHONE!"

"I heard you!" Beth stumbled into the hallway.

"YOU DON'T NEED TO YELL!" Lisa fell into an injured silence.

If I'm lucky, she won't talk to me for the rest of the morning, Beth thought as she lifted the receiver.

"I HEARD THAT!"

Beth suppressed the urge to scream, then said, "Hello?"

"Beth? It's Judy. I'm so sorry, it just wasn't possible to make it back for Mom's funeral. Besides, I didn't know if I'd be welcome."

Beth recognized the tone of voice. It was all at once patronizing, slick, syrupy, and tinged with just the right amount of guilt.

"And poor Ernesto dying on the same day. I don't know how you coped," Judy said.

Beth heard Atlantic waves. She closed her eyes and thought for a moment. A part of her longed for sand and salt water sifting around her ankles. If she played it just right, Judy might invite her down. Beth shook her head and said, "What do you want?"

"Pardon me?"

Beth heard the real Judy. The Judy who always got what she wanted. "This is the way you talk to me when you want something. So, what do you want?" Beth said.

Lisa appeared in the doorway, "DON'T YOU TALK TO MY MOTHER LIKE THAT!"

Beth turned her head and stared, momentarily freezing Lisa with a glare.

"I'VE GOT SUCH BAD CRAMPS!" Lisa said, held her stomach, and retreated into the bathroom.

You can still hear what we say from the bathroom, Beth thought.

"Is Lisa okay?" Judy said.

If you're so concerned, why isn't she with you? Beth thought.

Judy said, "It's so good of you to take her in for me. I don't blame you for being upset with me for missing the funeral, but we're all that's left of the family. We're still sisters."

"Do you want to talk to Lisa?"

"Oh no, we need to talk. Like sisters. Like we used to."

"Talk?" Beth said.

"Well, you know, this business opportunity came up on the island and I just couldn't turn it down."

"Bob show up yet?" Beth said.

"Not a hair."

Beth was sure she heard relief in her sister's voice. "We haven't seen him either. Lisa would like to talk with you."

"I don't want to bother her," Judy said.

"You sure?"

"Look," Judy said.

Here it comes. The bottom line, Beth thought.

"They're attempting to freeze my assets." Judy was all business now.

"I thought only the daiquiris were frozen in the tropics," Beth said.

"It's no joke. There's an investigation."

"What kind of investigation?"

"Something to do with the RCMP and the divorce," Judy said.

"Divorce?" Beth said.

"Bob and I got divorced a little over a month ago."

Beth thought for a moment. Up to a couple of months ago, Judy's only assets had been a house with a second mortgage and a car dealership that was slowly going bankrupt. She decided to push Judy a little harder. "Then, why did you phone us to find out where he was?"

"Forget about that. I want my share of the inheritance."

You won't be happy with the will, Beth thought. An idea blossomed. "She did leave some money. How do I get it to you?"

"Well, it's complicated."

She expected me to put up more of a fight, Beth thought. "I've got to have some kind of address if I'm going to send it."

"It has to remain absolutely confidential."

Beth reached for a pen and wrote down the address. "You like living on the beach?"

"What did Lisa tell you?"

"I can hear the surf, Judy."

"Oh."

"I'm sure Lisa would like to talk with you," Beth said.

"I can't right now. Send her my best. How soon will you be sending the money?"

"I'll get right on it."

"Thanks. Bye." Judy hung up.

"Okay." Beth set the receiver down. "Lisa, have you got a passport?"

"YES."

Beth moved to the hallway. Through the bedroom doorway, she saw Ernie's empty bed. "Where's Ernie?"

"HOW WOULD I KNOW WHERE HE IS? HE'S NOT MY BROTHER."

❧

Ernie pressed the toe of his left runner against the heel of his right. Somehow, a pebble had hitched a ride inside his shoe. He balanced on one foot. Scout pulled. He ended up on his knees next to a red minivan with tinted glass.

"Scout!" Ernie pulled on the leash. "Sit!" He did the same. Lifting the running shoe, he turned it upside down and watched the pebble fall out. "Now, where were we going?" he said while pulling his runner on.

The van's fan whirred.

Why is its engine running? Ernie thought.

The van's side door slid open.

Scout's hair rose up. She growled and backed away.

"Wait." The voice came from inside the van. The man seemed to fill the interior.

Ernie felt his mouth fall open and the sweat on his back chilled the length of his spine. It couldn't be Uncle Bob, he thought. "No way."

The van's front door opened. A woman stepped out. Her hair was blond, gelled, and cut short. She wore a yellow tank top and a pair of black shorts with bulky military pockets. She opened the rear hatch.

There were goose bumps all along Ernie's arms and he started to shiver. His mind reeled with memories of Uncle Bob.

Scout barked a warning as the man stepped onto the sidewalk. His white shirt stuck to his flesh. He had black hair and a salt-and-pepper beard.

Ernie thought, If it weren't for the beard, he'd look just like, "Uncle Bob?" Ernie choked on the words.

The big man stood. His fly was open. One white shirt-tail peeked out.

Big man took a step closer.

Scout barked.

The man stepped back. "Hey, Annie, grab some cheese outta my bag!"

Ernie's wrist and elbow ached from the strain of holding Scout's leash. "Uncle Bob?"

"I'm Ralph Devine," Big man said.

"Here it is," Annie hefted the camera to her shoulder and tossed a bag of cheese.

Ernie couldn't seem to get enough oxygen.

"You're Ernie Rapozo." Ralph fumbled with the bag, pulled out a piece of cheese and broke it in half. He offered it to Scout.

She sniffed the treat.

Ernie saw the shirt-tail retract from Ralph's fly. "How do you know my name?"

Ralph smiled. "It's our job to know. We just want to ask you some questions. No harm in that?"

Ernie couldn't stop shivering.

Scout growled as Ralph took a half step forward.

"You gettin' this?" Ralph said to his partner.

"Rolling," Annie crouched for a lower angle of the boy and the dog.

"Have you seen Bob Swatsky recently?" Ralph said. He opened his hand. Scout inched forward, then retreated without taking the cheese. Ralph closed his fist. "Come on baby." With his other hand, he motioned Annie closer.

Ernie said, "How come it's so cold?"

"You gotta be kiddin'," Ralph said.

Ernie watched sweat form along Ralph's hairline.

Annie moved onto the grass. Ralph moved toward Scout. He revealed the cheese. Scout turned toward Annie.

Ernie blinked. In that instant, he imagined a knife. Ernie opened his eyes.

"Hey, stop it!" Annie said.

"What's wrong?" Ralph kept his eyes on Ernie.

"Dog stuck his nose in my crotch." Annie pointed the camera at Scout.

"Her," Ernie said.

"What?" Ralph said.

"Scout's a she, not a he," Ernie said.

"Whatever." Annie pointed the camera at Ernie. "Tell 'her' to stop."

"You tell her," Beth said.

Ralph looked past Ernie. Annie pointed the camera at Beth striding up the sidewalk in a pink nightshirt.

"Mom, you aren't wearing a bra," Ernie said.

"Where'd you go? I woke up and you were gone." Beth leaned to help Ernie to his feet.

"Took the dog for a walk. Lisa was snoring. I couldn't sleep." Ernie swayed and Beth caught him around the shoulders.

"Do you know where Bob Swatsky is?" Ralph said. Annie moved in for a close-up.

"Who are you?" Beth said.

"Ralph Devine. v Channel. Do you know where Bob Swatsky is?"

"No." Then Beth said to Ernie, "What's the matter?"

"It's cold out here." Saliva collected at the back of his throat.

"Ernie, you on somethin'?" Devine said.

"Shit! Get your nose outta there!" Scout yelped and backed away. Annie tripped over a crack in the sidewalk.

The camera fell. Annie reached. It rolled away from her. "Ow!" The lens hit her toe before the camera toppled onto its side and scattered bits of plastic onto the sidewalk. "Stupid dog!"

Ernie leaned forward and heaved. Vomit spilled onto the sidewalk.

Devine stepped back, "My shoes!"

Ernie shivered uncontrollably.

"Ernie!" Beth said as she held him by the shoulders. She shifted a hand to his forehead.

Ernie heaved.

"Ernie!" Beth looked around, searching for help.

Devine picked up bits of the camera, "Think it'll still work?"

Annie said, "I'm callin' an ambulance, lady."

⌘

Beth said, "I don't want to leave a message. I want to talk with Detective Lane. Don't put me on hold. I don't want to talk with anyone else. I left his pager number at home in my purse. I left in a hurry. I'm in my nightshirt at the Foothills Hospital Emergency and I'm in no mood for any double talk." She repeated the doctor's questions in her mind, "Is your son depressed? Have his sleeping patterns altered? Is he eating? Has he lost weight? Any problems at home?" She looked above the phone. The sign read "Have You Been Sexually Assaulted?" Below the sign was a list of numbers.

"We're trying to locate him," the male voice said.

"Thank you." Beth leaned forward. Tears rolled off the tip of her nose.

"All I'm saying is I'm considering it," Lane said. They sat at the back of the coffee shop. The walls were a forest green. Green and white checkered tablecloths matched green and white floor tiles. Lane sipped a black Colombian. Harper stirred a latte. The window at the other end of the shop overlooked the Stephen Avenue Mall.

Harper said, "It goes against everything we've been taught."

"Yes, everything we're trained to do."

"Not just that. Look what's happened as a result of it," Harper said.

"The whole problem is my theory's based on a maximum of three witnesses. Two are dead. Now, there may only be one person who knows the whole story and he's not talking. If we threaten him or get tough, he'll clam up and we'll end up with less than we've got now."

"The theory matches the facts." Harper leaned back in his chair.

"Then, how do we prove it?"

"The location of the body seems the obvious place to start. And it's the location that makes it all so damned complicated. How'd you think of it?"

"Went to Hawaii when I was a kid. Took a guided tour of Oahu. The Vietnam War was still going on and there was a military cemetery. The army came up with a way to save space when the cemetery started to fill up." His cell phone rang. "Lane here. She still on the line? Give her my cell number and ask her to call." Lane looked at Harper. "It's Beth."

The cell phone rang. "Beth?"

Beth said, "Yes. Ernie's in emergency. He's still having flashbacks. He's not eating. This morning some reporters tried to talk to him and we ended up here."

Lane reached into his jacket pocket and pulled out a notebook. "Slow down. Are the doctors with him now?"

"They're waiting for the results of some more blood tests. They say it looks like his electrolytes are out of whack. Whatever that means."

"Is he going to be admitted?" Lane said.

"They haven't decided yet, besides, I don't think it's about his blood."

You're wrong there, this is all about blood and relatives, Lane thought. "How can I help?"

"What do you know? All I know, and I'm not even sure why I know, is that I need to know what my mother and Ernesto hid from us. You have a pretty good idea. So, what happened to Bob?"

"I don't know, exactly."

"Can we just get to the point? Either Ernie and I find out what's happened or I'm afraid he'll only get worse. They're talking about some kind of traumatic stress disorder."

"What's it been like for you two at home?" Lane said.

"He's not sleeping. Hardly eats anything. It's worse since my niece moved in," Beth said.

"Bob's daughter?" Lane remembered Lisa handing out her business cards at the funeral.

"That's right. But it's all about to change."

"When?"

"As soon as I can make an airline reservation and call her a cab," Beth said.

"Cayman Islands?"

"Yes."

"Can you move?" Lane said.

"What?"

"Can you move out of your mother's house?"

"Where would we go?" Beth asked.

"Not very far," Lane said.

CHAPTER 26

"How's Randy going to help us if he won't talk?" Harper asked.

Lane turned the wheel and eased into the west entrance of Queen's Park Cemetery. Harper looked out the side window. The new detective rubbed his palms on beige cotton trousers and shifted his shoulders around inside the jacket. Then, he reached for his belt to adjust his new Glock hand gun.

"Randy's smart and it's hard to predict how he'll react." Lane wanted to ease the tension between them.

The lines at the corners of Harper's eyes and mouth looked like they'd been stretched tighter. The muscles of his jaw worked under the skin. His mustache twitched.

I've gone too far, Lane thought. Treated him like he's a rookie.

"What's he look like?" Harper said.

"Over six feet. Lean. Walks like a jock. Has a red hard hat. Usually, he's around the mausoleum." They passed the grey concrete building. No sign of Randy. The road descended. Trees sprinkled the car with shade. "There." Lane pointed at the man kneeling at a grave. Randy's hands were up to the wrists in loam. Nearby trees stretched at least ten metres high. As they eased closer, they saw a bag of wildflower seeds. Randy bent forward revealing the name on the gravestone.

"Ernesto's?" Harper said.

"Yep." Lane flicked the toggle switch on the door's armrest. His window slid down. He stopped and turned off the engine.

Randy turned and looked at them. Then he lifted an orange marigold in a plastic pot and turned it upside down.

His left hand righted the plant and he set it in a hollow scooped out of the loam. He packed soil around the plant before easing back on his heals, standing and leaning to pick up a watering can. With a graceful back and forth motion, he sprinkled water over the grave. Setting the watering can down, he turned. The knees of his work pants were stained black. Randy brushed at them with his hands, then bent to wipe his palms on the grass over Helen's grave. "He used to call this rubbing her back. Ernesto liked flowers so much, I thought it would be nice to plant some perennials."

Lane opened the Chev's door and stepped out, "We've got a bit of a problem." He looked past Randy to the A frame building further up the hill.

"Don't worry about Tony. If we move away, he'll just get more suspicious. If we act like we're having a conversation, he'll get out the binoculars. He says he can read lips, but he says lots of things that aren't true." Randy lifted the hard hat and wiped his forehead.

Harper stood at the front of the car.

"This is Detective Harper, my partner."

Randy stared for a moment, looked at Lane, then back at Harper. "Read something about you. A few years back you were shot in the leg and another officer saved your life. Lane was never formally recognized." He smiled at Harper's obvious discomfort. "I must say this is a surprise."

"Surprising things happen," Lane said, determined not to allow Randy to take control of the conversation this time. "We're here to deal with the present. Ernie's depressed and sleep deprived. He's having trouble eating. Some reporter tried to talk with him this morning and the boy ended up in hospital. Beth thinks it might have something to do with the sexual assault."

Randy frowned.

"Since we haven't been able to locate Bob Swatsky, Ernie thinks it's only a matter of time before his uncle comes back to finish the job." Lane leaned back against the car.

"Anybody think to get the kid a shrink?" Randy said.

Lane watched Randy's eyes. Let him work it over for a second, Lane thought before he said. "I've got a theory about what happened and one living witness who won't talk. I figure Ernie's telling the truth. And I've got another problem." He indicated Harper. "My partner thinks hiding the truth only makes the situation worse. Thinks it's our job to find out what happened and it's up to the courts to decide after that.

"I figure this reluctant witness won't talk no matter what. Either he knows he'll lose his job because he helped dispose of the body or he figures telling what he knows will hurt someone else. That leaves us all with one big problem. Ernie. What do we do about the boy?" Lane looked at the graves. "Ernesto wanted to take care of the boy. Leona wanted to do the same. Beth wants help for her son. She's afraid she's going to lose him."

Randy said, "He knows all of it?" He looked at Harper.

"That's right," Harper said.

"You're big on the public's right to know?" Randy said to Harper.

"No, just big on the truth," Harper said.

Lane suppressed a smile. Good move, he thought.

Randy said, "The way I see it, the truth gets lost when ratings and money are involved. The more sensational the story, the bigger the ratings. The truth gets twisted and a kid who's already in rough shape can become a basket case. Reporters will turn his world upside down."

"Lying to protect Ernie hasn't done him much good so far," Harper said.

Randy said, "So, either way, the kid gets hurt. I guess the question really is whether or not you think we have the right to determine how badly he gets hurt."

"Beth and Ernie are going to have something to say about this," Lane said.

"Then bring them here." Randy made it sound like a challenge.

⁂

"v Channel News at six." The anchor stared into the camera. Her shoulder length blond hair was parted down the middle. Her white blouse was buttoned to the throat. "Reporter Ralph Devine has a story about the perils a journalist faces while getting to the bottom of a story."

A head and shoulders shot of Ralph smiling into the camera, "Getting the story can be a little dangerous."

Cut to a shot of Scout barking, teeth bared.

A shot of Beth's angry face. She said, "You tell her."

Cut to Ernie on the ground.

Cut to Ralph with a broken camera on the hood of a v Channel van. "v Channel refuses to be intimidated by those who would attempt to hide the truth behind the disappearance of Bob Swatsky."

The anchor's eyes narrowed as she turned to face the camera. "Reporter Ralph Devine will continue to dig for the truth behind the disappearance of Bob Swatsky. Swatsky is wanted for questioning by the RCMP and Calgary police. It's believed he holds the key to a land scam involving an estimated 15 million dollars."

CHAPTER 27

"What do I do about the TV crew parked outside?" Beth used the phone in her kitchen.

"Your niece gone yet?" Lane said.

"In the shower. Her taxi'll be here any minute."

"What about Ernie?"

"Just got up. Watching TV. He's got a blank look on his face. It scares me. The doctor said he needs rest and regular meals. We have to wait six weeks for an appointment with some specialist. How can we live like this for six weeks?"

Can he handle what Randy will have to say? Lane thought. "We'll be there in five minutes. We'll handle the TV crew."

"The car's all packed. The lawyer told me to lock up the house and leave it. He'll take care of the rest."

"Good."

"Just have to give Miguel a call," Beth said.

"What?"

"I've left it to last for a reason."

"But—" It's too important to leave to the last, Lane thought.

"He won't be able to talk me out of it now. The decision's made." She looked at the wall where the picture of her mother and father had hung. It was packed away in a suitcase in the trunk of the Dodge.

"I'll call when we get there," Lane said.

"Thanks." Beth hung up.

Lisa was singing in the shower. "LEAVIN' ON A JET PLANE." The words to the song stopped when she gargled.

Beth reached into the watch pocket of her jeans, pulled out a folded piece of paper and opened it. She tapped a series of numbers.

The phone rang twice before an exotic female voice said, "Miguel Rapozo's Tunisia office."

"Connect me with Miguel. Please." It's way after office hours over there, she thought.

"I'm sorry. Miguel, I mean Mr. Rapozo, is in a meeting. Can I take a message?"

"It's a family emergency," Beth said.

"DON'T KNOW WHEN I'LL BE BACK AGAIN," Lisa sang.

"Another one?" The secretary's tone was a mixture of skepticism, condescension, and sarcasm.

"That's correct," Beth said.

"A moment."

Beth patted her pocket, checking for car keys and the envelope. Inside the envelope were two thousand dollar bills and a note explaining that Lisa's one-way plane ticket was paid for in cash. That was all. No warning that the lawyer was sending a copy of the will. No hint that the inevitable accusatory phone call from Judy would remain unanswered. By that time Beth and Ernie would be gone. She realized the note might well be their final contact. Beth felt a combination of release and regret. Just Ernie, Scout, and Beth. All that was left of her family. And she knew, for the first time, how Ernesto must have felt after the death of his wife.

"Hello?" Miguel was angry.

"Miguel." Beth felt angry at having to beg.

"Yep."

"Ernie's sick. We're moving into Nonno's house. You can reach him there," Beth said.

"You sure that's wise?" Miguel said.

Sure I'm sure, she thought, Do you think I'd come crawling to you if I wasn't sure? Instead she said, "Yes."

"All right, then."

"And we're going to be needing the van," Beth said.

"Up to you," Miguel said.

She heard the dismissal in his tone of voice. That had been the way of it. It was up to her to take care of their son, up to her to make the funeral arrangements, up to her to turn a blind eye to his affairs. Always, up to her. "Goodbye," she said.

She went upstairs to the door of her mother's room. The bed was a confused mass of pillows and rumpled sheets. Lisa's denim purse perched at the foot of the mattress. The purse was open. Pink sanitary napkins and wads of thousand dollar bills lay side by side. What the hell is Lisa doing with all that money? Beth thought.

"LEAVINNNNN' ON A JET PLANE!"

Beth thought, Why is she waiting for an inheritance when she has all of that money? She shook her head as she moved past the bathroom to Ernie's door.

All the packing had been done after two this morning while Lisa snored. Beth had just finished at 4:00 AM when Ernie screamed himself awake.

Beth thought, Where did all of that money come from?

The shower stopped.

Beth moved for the stairway. She checked to see if she was about to trip over the oxygen line snaking its way up the stairs and into her mother's room. You don't need to do that anymore, she thought.

The carpet on the stairs rubbed the soles of her feet like a memory.

The sound of the television greeted her as she stepped off the bottom stair. "Orangutans have no need for human contact." In the background there was the grunting of an ape.

"PBS," Beth said to herself. Ernie stayed on the safe channels. One naturalist program after another. Lisa, on the other hand, spent every waking moment watching the news and interrogating Beth.

Beth stepped into the family room. Ernie sat in the easy chair with blank eyes staring at the screen. Scout was next to him. Her eyes were closed while both ears stayed erect and alert.

"Ernie?" Beth said.

He looked at her. Scout's eyes opened.

"We're leaving right after Lisa," Beth said.

Ernie smiled.

She looked at his belt. It was cinched two notches in from the old line worn across the leather. How much more weight will he lose in a week? she thought.

The doorbell rang.

Scout barked and bounded for the front door.

Beth followed, reached the door and peered through the peephole. The man in the fish eye had on a white shirt, tie, and jacket. She opened the door part way. Scout growled.

"Taxi," the man said.

"She'll be right out."

"Been waitin' five minutes already," the driver said.

"Sorry." Beth shut and locked the door. "Lisa, the taxi's here."

"ALREADY?"

"It's been here for five minutes," she said.

"I HEARD THAT!"

Beth cursed under her breath, "Bullshit." Bent low, holding Scout's collar, she walked to the family room. "Ernie, take care of the dog." Scout jumped up and licked his face.

At the back door, Beth lifted Lisa's blue bag. "Try travelling light, Lisa." She unlocked the back door and opened the screen. She took quick short steps down the driveway where concrete burned the soles of her feet. Looking beyond the black taxi, she saw the van with v Channel stenciled on the hood. Beth heard the van's door slide open when she stepped to the back of the taxi. Using both hands, she heaved Lisa's bag into the trunk.

Hopping off the pavement, onto the sidewalk and then the cooler grass, Beth looked across the street. A man backed out of the van's side door. The driver's door opened. Ralph Devine raised an arm and pointed at her, "Ms. Rapozo, a moment of your time."

She turned and, in spite of panic and the burning concrete, walked at a steady pace, stepped through the gate and closed it behind her.

"You'll have to talk to me sooner or later!" Devine said.

Beth stepped inside the house, making sure to lock the inside door. "Lisa!"

"WHAT!" Lisa stood in the hallway with wet, straight hair. She rummaged through her denim purse. "WHERE'S MY TICKET?"

Beth kept her voice free of any sarcasm, "It's in your hand."

"NO WAY!" Lisa glared back before glancing at the ticket in her left hand. "OH."

"Taxi's waiting," Beth said.

"I KNOW!" Lisa pushed past in a cloud of peach perfume.

The scent caught at the back of Beth's throat. She reached into her pocket and pulled out the envelope addressed to Judy. "This is for your mother."

Lisa turned, spied the envelope and snatched it. "MY INHERITANCE!" She stuffed the ticket into her bag.

Beth watched, knowing what would happen next.

Lisa ripped the envelope in half. Peering into one half, she reached in and pulled out half of two $1000 bills. "WHY DIDN'T YOU TELL ME THERE WAS MONEY INSIDE?"

"It's for your mom." Beth pushed the fingers of her right hand through her hair.

"THAT'S ALL?" Lisa peered into the other half of the envelope.

"More than you deserve." The words were out before Beth could think.

"I CAN'T BELIEVE YOU SAID THAT! AFTER ALL THAT'S HAPPENED TO ME, I JUST CAN'T BELIEVE IT!"

"Believe it, sweetie." Beth crossed her arms and leaned against the door frame.

"I'M NEVER COMING BACK HERE!" Lisa turned toward the back door. She jammed her feet into red open-toed shoes with seven centimetre heels. "WHERE'S MY LUGGAGE?"

"In the taxi," Beth said.

"IT BETTER BE!" Lisa yanked at the door, stopped, turned the dead bolt and heaved. The doorknob punched a hole in the drywall. Beth was left with a cloud of peach perfume.

The front doorbell rang.

Scout barked.

Beth opened the back door screen just long enough to watch Lisa slam the gate, scuff her heels down the driveway, and step up to the side of the taxi. She climbed inside.

A Chevy Blazer pulled out from behind the v Channel van.

The taxi pulled away.

The Blazer followed.

A black-haired man peered around the side of the garage.

Beth stepped inside and locked both doors.

The front doorbell rang again.

Scout barked.

"Shit!" Beth moved down the hall to the front door and looked through the peephole. The fish-eye face of Ralph Devine peered back at her.

The phone rang. Beth ran for the kitchen.

Ernie sat, staring at the TV and holding onto Scout's collar.

"Can't you get the phone?" Beth said.

Ernie's surprise faded into a blank stare. He turned back to the TV.

Ernie won't even fight, Beth thought. I wish he would fight back. She picked up the phone, "Hello?"

"We're outside."

"Lane?"

"Yes. We're ready whenever you are."

"Thanks." The tears started as Beth hung up. She sat at the kitchen table with her hands between her knees and felt her shoulders shake. Something cool and wet touched her hand. She looked down. Scout looked back at her. "Thanks girl." Beth smiled.

A hand touched her shoulder. "You okay, Mom?"

She looked at Ernie then leaned till her head touched him.

Ernie said, "Don't worry."

The doorbell rang.

Scout barked and scampered for the front door.

Beth felt like she might start to laugh and never stop. "We have to go."

"Want me to answer the door?" Ernie said.

"No. Just turn off the TV."

A shadow appeared behind the curtains covering the sliding glass door. Knuckles rapped on the glass.

"Don't answer it." Beth looked around the kitchen. She saw her mother leaning over the sink. Her mother took a pull on a cigarette. Beth shook away the memories, pushed the chair in and stood to watch the silhouette behind the curtain. "Get Scout and we'll get in the car."

"Come on, girl," Ernie said.

Scout bounded into the kitchen and barked at the silhouette.

Beth turned to see if the stove was off. She opened the fridge. Empty.

"Let's go," Ernie said.

Beth walked through the family room to the door of the attached garage. Inside, the light in the belly of the garage door opener cast long shadows. Ernie held Scout's leash in his left hand. He opened the car's back door and shut it after Scout jumped inside.

Beth reached into her pocket for keys.

The passenger door's hinge squeaked.

Beth said, "I forgot my shoes."

Someone pounded on the garage door.

Beth got in and wrapped ten toes over top of the brake pedal. The twenty-five-year-old engine coughed and caught.

Beth said, "Ernie, the garage door opener."

He reached, pressed the button. Light flooded inside.

Beth shifted into reverse. Left hand on the wheel, right hand on the back of the seat, she looked out the rear window.

The garage door rose above the height of the trunk.

Beth eased her foot off the brake.

Ralph Devine peered under the door. On the other side, the dark-haired man lifted a TV camera to his shoulder.

"Just a few questions!" Devine said.

Beth concentrated on driving. The men on either side were shadows in her peripheral vision. A line of shade passed over the car.

"Shut the garage door," Beth said.

The rear bumper scraped pavement as they bounced onto the street. She stepped on the brake, shifted into drive, and looked ahead.

The camera man stepped off the curb and aimed his camera at Beth.

She turned the wheel to the left. "God I wish this car had power steering." She eased forward.

The cameraman stepped back and fell backwards over the curb.

"I'll get blamed for that," Beth said. The engine shuddered, nearly stalling. She curved her toes over the top of the accelerator and pushed gently. The engine smoothed out. They passed the cameraman aiming his lens at Ernie. Scout bared her teeth, barking fog and saliva onto the window.

The car laboured its way up to fifty kilometres per hour. In the rear-view mirror, Beth saw Ralph Devine following the cameraman as they headed for the van.

⚜

Lane and Harper watched from behind a parked pickup truck. "Looks like we only have to worry about one vehicle," Lane said.

Harper grabbed his notebook and flipped to a fresh page.

Lane pulled out to follow the van. "You still don't like this."

"No." Harper plucked a pen from his shirt pocket. "Giving a reporter, especially this guy, a ticket doesn't bother me. It's the rest of it I don't like."

"Ever been close to a story Devine covered?" Lane matched his speed with the van's to keep a block between them. Remember, he thought, you know where Beth's headed, they don't.

"Couple of times," Harper said.

"Did he ever get at the truth?"

"Not even close."

Lane nodded, "Lots of people in town think he's great. Think he should run for mayor." Lane watched the van run a stop sign. "Get that?"

Harper looked at his watch and wrote down the time. Then he read the street sign as they stopped at the corner. He wrote it down as well. "It's not about V Channel's reporting," Harper said. "So far, we've got four deaths. If you're right, then we're dealing with five. Our job is to gather evidence and lay charges, not play judge and jury."

Lane watched the van pull up behind Beth's antique Dodge. Overhead, the trees lining Northmount Drive reached to touch one another. "Ever meet a fifteen-year-old who goes into jail and comes out ten years later?"

"No."

Lane tapped his temple with a finger, "Gets out and is still fifteen up here."

"This kid's not going to jail. Besides, that's not our problem."

"Whose problem is it, then?" Lane said.

"The court's."

"And if we don't gather all of the facts, then a decision is made on limited information. At least this way, two more people are going to know what happened. At least, that is, if Randy will tell them what he knows. His relationship with Ernesto obliges him to do that," Lane said.

"Or it obliges him to lie and cover up what happened. Isn't the van following a little too close?"

"Got to be less than a car length."

Harper glanced at his watch, noted the street running across Northmount and scribbled in his book. "I still think we should take Randy in for questioning and see what happens."

"He's expecting that." Ahead, yellow lights flashed over a pedestrian crossing. A woman with a baby carriage waited on the curb. Beth braked. The V Channel van locked its rear wheels. Blue smoke boiled around the tires. The van slid sideways. Lane smelled burnt rubber. The mother pushed her child across the street. She glared at the driver of the van.

"Close," Harper said. He noted time and location. Beth pulled ahead and the van followed. "Questioning Randy can't hurt."

"Randy's going to turn any interrogator inside out. After that, we'll get nothing," Lane said.

"Then you do the questioning."

"He's already told me as much as he's going to tell."

Harper said, "We got enough on the van?"

"I think so. Besides we're getting close to the cemetery. Beth will be getting nervous."

Harper radioed information to a blue and white patrol car waiting further along Northmount Drive.

They stopped at the lights on 14th Street.

The light turned green. Beth led them through the intersection. Harper pointed at the strip mall on the south side of Northmount. A police cruiser waited in the parking lot. "There she is."

The blue and white accelerated out of the parking lot. The cruiser's overhead lights flashed. The siren sounded. Beth pulled over. The v Channel van parked behind her. The cruiser stopped and an officer stepped out, made eye contact with Harper and nodded. Harper nodded back. "We're gonna owe her big time. The reporter's gonna give her an earful."

"And she'll enjoy every minute of it. Writing up tickets for reporters was always fun." Lane passed Beth and she followed. Northmount curved south and out of the v Channel van's line of sight. Lane turned left up a hill. He looked in the mirror. She was there.

Beth smiled, recalling the look on the face of the cameraman. The moment he realized the police officer was stopping him, the cameraman had mouthed one four-letter word.

The air flowing in through her open window made the heat bearable. Beth followed Lane's grey Chev past a no dogs sign, through the gate to Queen's Park Cemetery, and along the pavement running between two rows of evergreens. The road tipped down into the valley. The Chev's brake lights came on and Lane pulled to the side of the road. Beth stopped two car lengths behind.

"I think he wants you to pull alongside," Ernie said.

Beth spotted Lane's left hand waving them ahead. Her nerves tingled. "Damn steering." She heaved on the wheel and stopped next to the unmarked car. "Thanks for getting rid of the TV crew."

Lane jerked his right thumb in his partner's direction. "He did it."

Harper leaned forward and smiled.

"Randy told me to park over there." Lane pointed at the oblong concrete structure to the right. "He wants you to follow that road to the left and he'll meet you in Section J, Block 25."

"Section J, Block 25," Beth said. She released the brake and turned left. Within 100 metres, they spotted a yellow tractor with its bucket scooping earth. The operator sat up top while another man shovelled soil over a fresh grave.

"What's Randy look like now?" Ernie said.

Beth saw that Scout had her chin on Ernie's right shoulder. The dog licked the breeze with her tongue. "Looks something like one of those guys on the cover of a magazine. You knew him when you were little."

Ernie smiled at his mother's description of Randy.

Embarrassment rose up Beth's neck.

Gravestones came close to the edge of the road on either side. Ahead, an artillery piece was aimed at the centre of town.

They passed through an intersection and the road curved to the right.

The slope was dotted with willows whose lazy limbs brushed headstones. Near the graves, peonies sprouted in pinks and reds.

"Creepy," Beth said.

"Kind of pretty," Ernie said.

They passed a squat, green vehicle with John Deere and Gator stamped on its sides. A blue cooler sat in the back of the Gator.

"That him?" Ernie pointed at a man in a red hard hat guiding a Weed Eater through the long grass around the base of a tree. Randy looked up. The gas engine slowed to idle and sputtered before stopping. Leaning the weed trimmer against his ribs, Randy pulled at earplugs.

Beth stopped. "That's him."

Randy smiled and waved.

Scout barked.

Ernie opened his door.

Scout jumped over the back seat, onto Ernie's lap and outside.

"Scout!" Beth said as she shut off the engine.

A gopher ran and hopped across the pavement. Scout pounded along behind.

The gopher disappeared down a hole. Another gopher whistled. Scout raced from one hole to the next.

Randy strolled closer. "She's okay. Let her run. Not many people around this time of day."

"You sure?" Beth watched the dog stick its nose down a hole.

"Will she stay close?" Randy said.

"Always keeps us in sight."

"Then, there's no problem." Randy moved to the Gator and set the weed trimmer in the back. "Ernie? Help me with this, will you?" Randy grabbed one of the cooler's handles and waited.

Ernie grabbed the other handle. They walked across the grass with the cooler between them. Beth followed to a bench speckled by the shade of an elm. I hope this will help Ernie, she thought.

"Time for lunch," Randy said. They set the cooler down by the bench.

"We didn't come for a picnic," Beth said.

"The truth tastes better with good food. Ernesto told me that when I first came here. I thought he was crazy. He found out I wasn't bringing a lunch, so he brought one for me. He fed me and then he listened when I started to talk. Now it's my turn to return the favour. You came here to find out what I know and I'll tell you, but it's important to eat." Randy lifted the lid of the cooler. "Want a pop?"

"Sure." Ernie accepted a can and pulled back the tab.

"Beth?" Randy said.

"Please." She rolled the can's cool surface across her forehead and sat on the end of the bench.

"Sandwich?" Randy gave each a cellophane wrapped bun. "Hope you like cheese, lettuce, and pastrami.

"Our last meal?" Beth said.

"Or your first." Randy sat down and leaned his back against the trunk of the elm.

"I'm not really hungry." Ernie sipped his pop.

"After Bob was through with you, one of the emotions you felt was helplessness. Helplessness because someone took control of your life and there wasn't much you could do about it."

Ernie said, "How did you know?"

"I've been there. Now you have a choice. I'm asking you to eat. All you have to do is listen. You can get up and leave any time you want or you can sit, eat, and listen."

Ernie crossed his ankles and sat. He put the pop between his legs, unwrapped the end of the bun and took a bite.

Randy lifted his pop. "Ernesto came here the morning Bob attacked you. It was a Tuesday?"

"Yes," Ernie said.

Beth nodded and realized how hungry she was when she bit into the bun and tasted the fresh-baked bread.

"Ernesto was driving a Lincoln. Helen was in the passenger seat. He didn't see me. It was coffee time and I was leaning up against this tree. You get to know someone real well when you work alongside him day after day. The way Ernesto moved when he got out of the car, I could tell there was something wrong. There was something about his posture. And he didn't usually show up at that time of day." Randy took another sip. "See those two willows?" He pointed at a pair of trees with white limbs and leaves hanging close to the ground. "The backhoe was down there. See the large headstone in black? The one shaped like a cross."

Beth and Ernie looked down over the tops of rows of gravestones and into the valley. One headstone stood out among the others. It was under a hill of fresh earth dotted with Canadian and American flags.

Randy said, "One of the other guys had just about finished up the hole but was gone for coffee. Ernesto was real careful to back the car up close to the hole. Then he climbed into the backhoe and started digging. I wondered why he went so deep. It all made sense when he eased the backhoe's bucket over to the rear of the Lincoln. He got down off the tractor, pulled a rope out of the trunk and tied it to the bucket. It was kind of slick the way he used the bucket to lift the body out of the trunk. For a moment it just hung there. Even from up here I could see the dead guy's fly was open. Ernesto eased the body into the bottom of the hole, climbed out of the cab and cut the rope. He pulled a couple of bags out of the trunk and a big sheet of plastic. He dumped the bags into the hole. Then he refilled part of it and used the bucket to flatten the bottom. That way nobody would know what he'd done. The backhoe operator joked later on about how one hole had dug itself. He looked at me like I'd played a practical joke on him. I played along."

Ernie looked at his sandwich. One bite was left. "Uncle Bob. It had to be him."

Beth put her arms around her belly and looked at her son. She felt sick with the certainty of what must come next.

"For the rest of that day and that night I tried to figure out what kind of mess Ernesto was in. The next day, I read about what happened to you. Then, it all made sense," Randy said.

Beth said, "My mother must have called Ernesto. All he had to do was back the Lincoln into the garage and drag Bob down the hall. Then Mom called the ambulance for Ernie."

"That's what Ernesto said when I asked him three days later. He told me that Leona had been asleep upstairs, heard a noise, and found Ernie and Bob on the floor. Bob was dead and she couldn't get Ernie to wake up. Leona phoned Ernesto for help. When he got there, they rolled Bob over. His pecker was hanging out of his pants and the knife was on the floor. They put two and two together. Leona cleaned some of the blood off Ernie's face and they decided the best thing to do was look out for their grandson."

"So, he's not coming back?" Ernie looked first to Beth and then to Randy for confirmation.

Beth opened her mouth to speak then said to herself, What will Ernie do when he figures it out?

"I don't have to worry," Ernie stared down into the valley at the headstone.

"Who else knows?" Beth said. Fear scratched its nails along her spine.

"The three of us and Lane." Randy watched Ernie and waited.

"He knows?" Beth put her hand over her mouth.

"Lane suspects, but his hands are tied without proof," Randy said.

"All he has to do is exhume the body." Beth's mind raced as she tried to think ahead.

"Two bodies, actually, and that creates a bit of a problem," Randy said.

"Who else is buried there?" Beth said.

"You wouldn't believe me if I told you."

"Who?" Ernie said.

Randy told them.

"You've got to be kidding!" Beth said.

"Nope."

"Lane will still get the body exhumed." Beth looked at her son as she said the words.

"Won't do him much good." Randy drained his pop. "Not now."

❧

Ernie chewed the last bite of his second sandwich then licked his fingers.

Beth put her foot to the floor and tried the engine again. It coughed, cleared its throat, and caught. A cloud of black smoke puffed from the tailpipe.

"This old girl doesn't like the heat," Randy crouched on Ernie's side of the car.

"Doesn't like the cold, either," Ernie said.

Beth said, "Thanks, Randy, for everything."

Randy lifted his hand, fingers open, cocked his head to one side and said, "Forget it. Oh, I almost forgot." He pulled out a business card and handed it to Ernie. "She's a good doctor. Helped me deal with what happened. If you decide that's what you want, she's a good one to talk with."

Ernie took the card and tucked it into his pocket.

Beth pulled away. The car gathered speed as the road dropped into the bottom of the valley. She braked. They passed the grave with its metre-high black stone cross and the flags.

"Aren't we going to talk to Lane?" Ernie said.

Beth hit the brakes hard. Ernie put his hand against the dash. Scout yelped when she fell against the back of the front seat.

"Mom?"

She looked at her hands gripping the wheel. "Are you crazy?"

Ernie considered the question, "You think this will go away?"

She felt the flat of Ernie's hand between her shoulder blades.

"Uncle Bob's not coming back. You don't know how it feels to know he's not coming back."

"Do you know what it all means?" she said.

"What?"

"It probably means Bob is dead because you hit him."

"I just hit him once. He said he was gonna kill me if I didn't do what he said. He was gonna cut my nose off and then he was gonna cut my heart out."

"You didn't tell me all of it," Beth said.

"I didn't remember it all till later. It came back in bits and pieces. I remember the knife. I remember what he smelled like. I remember the fear. I remember hitting him. I remember falling. I know what he said."

"What if you end up in jail?" Beth said.

Ernie's expression told her he hadn't thought of that.

"You don't understand." Beth touched the smudges of fatigue underneath his eyes.

"You think the reporter is gonna give up? You think Lane will? Maybe you don't understand."

She looked ahead at the intersection. Turn east or turn west? she thought.

"I want this to be over. My dad would run. I don't want to end up like him," Ernie said.

&

Harper said, "Why not dig down beside the hole?"

Lane looked across at his partner. The Chev's air conditioner pumped a cool breeze. "What do you mean?"

"Are there any graves right beside it? I mean, maybe we can dig a hole down alongside. That way we might not have to get permission to disturb the other body."

"Never thought of that," Lane said.

They heard the sound of an engine labouring up the hill. It was followed by the blue hood of Beth's Dodge.

"Do we follow her if she doesn't stop?" Harper said. They watched Beth look their way and turn toward them. She backed in, leaving a parking space between her and the ghost car.

Ernie opened his door, grabbed the dog's leash, then waited for his mother to come around and join him.

"You have any idea how this is going to play out?" Harper said.

"Looks good so far," Lane said.

Scout's tongue hung almost to the ground.

Lane opened his window. He hitched his thumb and pointed at the back seat. "Want to cool off?"

Beth frowned at Lane's choice of words. Ernie opened the door behind Lane. "Okay if Scout gets in?" Without waiting for permission, the dog hopped in and sat to ponder the pair in the front. Ernie climbed in. The dog eased closer to the boy when Beth climbed in the other side.

"You okay, girl?" Ernie said to Scout. He looked at Lane and Harper, "She was chasing gophers."

Harper smiled.

"She need some water?" Lane leaned against the driver's door.

"Just gave her some," Beth said.

"We found out where Uncle Bob is," Ernie said.

A rush of emotions ran through Beth.

Harper studied Ernie.

Lane looked at the boy and said, "You know that what you say here can be used in a trial. Detective Harper is going to be taking notes."

Harper picked up his notebook and propped it on his knee.

Ernie kept his eyes on Lane.

"Do you want a lawyer?" Lane looked at Beth as he asked the question.

"Do we need one?" she said.

"You might," Lane said.

Ernie said, "I want to get this over with. Besides, you know most of it already."

"I don't want my kid to go to jail," Beth said.

Lane said, "Look, I'll keep the questions general and if you don't want to answer, you don't have to. Okay?"

Ernie nodded.

"You don't agree?" Lane said to Beth.

"He says this is what he wants. What else can I do?" She wiped her palms on the thighs of her jeans.

"You can say no," Lane said.

"Ask your questions." Ernie scratched the back of the dog's head.

Lane looked at the boy, "Have you remembered anything more about Bob Swatsky's assault?"

"I remember the knife, the smell of him, the threats, and hitting him here." Ernie used his free hand to tap the soft tissue at the base of his throat.

"You said threats. Specifically, what did he say?" Lane said.

"He said he'd cut my nose off and then he'd cut my heart out if I didn't get on my knees. He told me to suck his . . ."

Lane looked at Ernie then at Harper to see if his partner was keeping up with the notes.

"He threatened your life," Lane said.

"That's important?" Ernie said.

"Very." Lane thought for a moment. "Do you remember anything else?"

"Just that he fell on me and then I remember waking up in the hospital and seeing my Mom leaning over the bed."

"Nothing else?"

"Nope," Ernie said.

Lane chose his words carefully. "Now, you say you have reason to believe you know where Bob Swatsky is. You might not want to mention the names of anyone living if you decide to discuss his whereabouts."

What is he doing? Beth thought.

Ernie considered this for a moment. "Nonno dumped Uncle Bob's body in a grave. We can show you where."

"How do you know this?" Lane said.

Ernie looked at Beth.

"You see, I have to have a good reason if I go digging for a body." Lane continued to gauge their reactions and study their eyes.

Beth said, "A reliable source said we would find the body in a grave down the hill."

"Do you know the name on the headstone?" Lane said.

Beth and Ernie nodded.

Lane said the name.

Ernie said, "Yes, that's it."

"Do I have to go to jail, now?" Ernie said. "I might have killed my uncle."

Beth gripped her son's knee.

Harper spoke before Lane could, "We have to determine the cause of death before we proceed."

Lane looked at Harper, then at Beth and Ernie.

Harper said, "We don't know if Swatsky died from a blow to the throat, a heart attack, or if someone else killed him. In fact, we don't know the cause of death until we have the results of an autopsy. We are obliged to make a solid case before laying any charges. We also have to consider the fact that this was a situation where Ernie's life was in imminent danger."

I couldn't have said it better, Lane thought.

CHAPTER 28

"v Channel morning news." The anchor's face was somber. "Reporter Ralph Devine has some shocking updates related to his ongoing coverage of the Swatsky saga."

Cut to a head and shoulders shot of Ralph Devine with the airport terminal in the background. "An exclusive interview with Lisa Swatsky, daughter of missing Red Deer Mayor Bob Swatsky, resulted in some startling revelations."

Cut to videotape of Lisa leaving the funeral home and waving at the camera.

Devine's voice-over continued, "Yesterday, a reporter talked with Ms. Swatsky as she waited for a flight to the Cayman Islands. Ms. Swatsky claims, and I quote, 'I delivered a bag of cash to the premier. My Dad told me it was part of a business deal.' When asked how much money was involved, she said, '$900,000, I think. I didn't count it all.'"

Cut to a head and shoulders portrait of a smiling Bob Swatsky. Devine said, "Lisa Swatsky is the daughter of Bob and Judy Swatsky. Judy recently divorced her husband and now lives in a million dollar mansion on the Cayman Islands. Officials believe Swatsky and his partners used money from an illegal land deal to buy real estate near this petrochemical plant."

Cut to a shot of smoke stacks and concrete buildings. "Investigators believe Swatsky bought the land after receiving insider information on plans for plant expansion. The land was sold for an estimated 15 million more than its purchase price."

Cut back to Ralph Devine, "When confronted with these allegations, the premier replied . . ."

Cut to the premier saying, "I want to know why Lisa Swatsky left the country only days after her father disappeared!"

Back to Devine. "We may never know what happened to Mayor Bob Swatsky and the missing money. Ralph Devine. v Channel News."

⁂

Arthur sat at his kitchen table and said, "Did you read this?" He dropped the folded front page of *The Calgary Herald* on the kitchen table. Its headline read "Premier Implicated in Swatsky Scandal."

Lane glanced at the clock on the stove. Just back from an early two hour walk around Glenmore Reservoir with Riley, he used a napkin to wipe the sweat from his forehead. Then he poured himself a cup of coffee. He glanced at the headline and said, "Not yet."

"The reporter maintains Lisa Swatsky told him she gave the premier a plastic shopping bag. And the bag contained close to $900,000."

Lane's eyebrows shifted, "Beth said Lisa had rolls of thousand dollar bills in her handbag. I wonder if the premier's shopping bag was a little short?"

"Lisa's statement about not counting the money was kind of odd."

"Lisa is odd," Lane said.

"Ernie might end up being a small part of a much bigger scandal."

"Or a bigger part, it's hard to tell."

"What do you mean?" Arthur said.

"You know how it goes. Some reporters like to speculate. The premier has already survived three scandals. Suspicion could easily shift to Ernesto, Leona, Beth, or Ernie. Who knows, somebody might even get the story right."

"Still, Judy living in the Cayman Islands in a million dollar mansion is sure to send some suspicion her way." Arthur rubbed Riley under the chin with his toe.

"Too early to tell. I'm heading for the shower."

The phone rang.

Arthur reached for it. "Hello? He's right here." He covered the mouthpiece and handed the phone to Lane, "Harper."

Lane took the phone, "Good morning." He listened intently before before saying, "Thanks." He handed the phone back to Arthur.

"Well?"

"He says the medical examiner may not be able to determine the exact cause of Bob Swatsky's death."

"The body was only there for two weeks," Arthur said.

"The body was covered with lime," Lane said.

"Lime?"

"If you choose the right kind of lime and know how to use it, it accelerates decomposition. They had to use dental records for a positive identification on the body. Very little was left except for bone, thirteen centimetres of zipper, spare change, a tie clip, cufflinks, and a wristwatch."

"Ernie's off the hook?" Arthur said.

"Even discounting self-defence, how could the Crown prove Ernie, Ernesto, Leona, or even heart failure was the cause of death? Apparently, Bob's heart wasn't in great shape. All we may have is interfering with a body—and the people responsible for that are already dead. The premier has suggested Lisa may be responsible for her father's disappearance. Next, she'll be accusing the premier. It looks like Beth and Ernie are last week's news."

CHAPTER 29

Ernie opened one eye. He was in his grandfather's house.

The phone rang.

He opened the other eye.

The phone rang again.

He lifted his feet out of tangled sheets, sat up and felt the cool touch of hardwood. His nose filled with the scent of fermenting wine.

The phone rang a third time.

He stood and stumbled into the hallway, then lifted the phone.

"Ernie?"

"Hi Mom."

"Did I get you out of bed?"

"Mmmhmmmm." He leaned his left arm against the wall and rested his head against his forearm.

"It's 10:30, Ernie."

"Mmmhmmmmm."

Scout stepped into the hallway, leaned on her front paws and stretched.

"You have to catch the 11:30 bus. Randy pulled some strings to get us an appointment. We can't miss it."

"I know."

"You went to bed at nine last night."

"I think so," Ernie said.

"And you slept right through?"

"Yeah."

"No . . . No dreams?"

"Nope."

"I'll see you at the doctor's office at one? I'm not taking my lunch hour till then, so you can't be late."

"Mom? How am I supposed to tell a stranger what happened?"

"We've been over this."

"I don't like it, Mom. What's she going to think?"

"Look, we agreed last night it was best to talk to someone who can help you. Help both of us."

"I don't know."

"Non me' rompere i coglioni," Beth said.

Ernie smiled at a memory of Nonno. Then, a flashback of his uncle and the knife pushed all other thoughts away.

CHAPTER 30

"That was Harper on the phone," Lane said. He stepped over Riley and onto the paving stones in their back yard. He wore shorts and a T-shirt. There won't be many more evenings like this, he thought. It was a little after eight and the sky was darkening. Across the alley, a few of the leaves on a poplar tree were beginning to yellow. Classical music and conversation from Mrs. Smallway's backyard created an oasis of noisy confidentiality for Lane and Arthur.

"What's new?" Arthur said and, "Thanks," when Lane set a sweating glass of beer on the table for each of them. Sweat also gathered on Arthur's forehead.

"They traced the Swatsky money. It all ended up in a numbered account in the Cayman Islands."

"So, Judy Swatsky pulled it off," Arthur said. Riley sauntered over and flopped. Arthur used his toe to rub the dog behind the ear.

"I can't help but think if I'd started talking with Ernie earlier on it would have helped the case and him," Lane said.

A particularly loud male voice from the yard next door said, "It works! Good God, Viagra works!"

Lane choked on his beer.

Arthur said, "They started when you were on the phone. It appears Mrs. Smallway is having a get-together. They just turned on the music. I can't believe it, they chose *Bolero*. The world is filled with injustice. Mrs. Smallway abuses perfectly good music, Ernie gets a shrink, and Judy gets 15 million."

"Actually, closer to sixteen. And, Canada has no extradition treaty with the Cayman Islands, so as long as Judy stays there, she'll be able to escape prosecution." Lane stretched his legs.

"Oh yes!" another voice said from Mrs. Smallway's yard.

"Want to go inside?" Lane said.

"Let's stay out here a little longer. It's too hot inside. Who knows, Mrs. Smallway's party might be worth a chuckle or two," Arthur said.

"Some lawyer in Red Deer is looking for ways to tie up Judy's money but it doesn't look promising."

"I talked with Beth Rapozo today. She and I both know what losing a family can be like. Beth was happy because Ernie gained four kilos. Come to think of it, Beth will probably be relieved that Judy can't be extradited."

"Why?" Lane said.

"Because neither Judy nor Lisa can come back to Canada. Beth and Ernie will be free of those two. Besides . . . "

"Who's next!" Mrs. Smallway said.

"Not me!" Arthur said. The voices next door went silent while *Bolero* played on.

Lane laughed.

Arthur said, " . . . that means Lisa can't leave either. She and her mother are stuck with each other."

Acknowledgments

For medical advice,
thank you
Bruce,
Colleen,
and Maureen.

For Italian translations,
thank you
Marie.

For great advice,
thank you
Cheryl.

Thank you
U of C
writer in residence,
Eden.

Don,
thank you
for the insights.

Policeman Gary,
thank you for
the tips.

Thanks to
creative writing students at
Lord Beaverbrook,
Alternative,
Forest Lawn, and
Queen Elizabeth
High Schools.

Thank you
Ruth
for the phone call and
Doug
for the editing.

GARRY RYAN was born and raised in Calgary, Alberta where he lives with his family. This first novel, *Queen's Park*, sprung from a desire to write a mystery with an emphasis on the rich diversity and unique locations of his hometown. He teaches English and Creative Writing to junior high and high school students, and in his spare time, he likes to take walks along the river with his dog, Scout. This is the first book in his Detective Lane mystery series.